Manfred's Folly

Timmon's Legacy

Author's Note

I was never sure where this book was going until the end of it. The new characters didn't walk in, sit down with me, drink tea, and tell me their stories. Instead, each discovery about them came as a surprise. The Shadow hovered tall over all the characters, as I surmised that there must be more endings to be dealt with. The stunning ending surprised me as much as it did the amazing characters involved in it. This book required scanty sips of early morning hot lemonade, sweet and tart. Cookies, too. Lots of them. And lots of pacing back and forth. If you enjoy a story where an accepted lifelong hopelessness is turned around in a startlingly quick and surprising act of intense redemption, I have tart lemonade and warm cookies ready and waiting for you.

Table of Contents

Manfred's Folly

Dere's bad bid'ness
goin' on over dere'!
Yep. bad bid'ness.
Best have yer'self handy
a mighty big prayer!

Chapter One

Louise Hope Cornfield

The First Day

Louise hope Cornfield drove the dusty, dying blue sedan gingerly into the driveway of the ratty little cottage. The sedan gave a last gasp and rattle as it floated to a stop. She sighed with relief. The long assed trip in the junk sedan was over.

She was here. Her new home. Just in time for yet another car funeral. Bone tired and thoroughly weary, she sat in the car, sunshine warming her tired bones while her eyes examined the cabin, the porch, and the old rusty station wagon parked under a huge tree with overhanging branches.

As Lou climbed out of the rusted out old junk car, a shadow passed through the sunshine, darkening everything around her. She stumbled backwards, almost going ass end over applecart. She righted herself and looked up. The shadow was gone. The sky had turned an incredible blue. Birds sang sweetly in the tall, green leafed trees, wooing their new tenant. High weeds gave off the familiar, dry, welcoming scent of childhood outdoor adventures.

Lou frowned. She detected magic here. Maybe good magic. Maybe bad. She sniffed the air. Well at least it smelt a hell of a lot better than the damned ol' car fumes she'd been breathin' in the last few hours.

She glanced at the rusty old station wagon sitting at the side of the cottage, almost hidden under the trees. It might be her next ride.

Yeah. There was magic here, all right. She'd just have to deal with it like she had countless times before.

Building up her courage, Lou trudged around the dead car, opened the trunk and pulled out her Goodwill suitcase. Slamming the trunk shut, she picked her way to the porch steps and climbed them, shrewd eyes darting everywhere. Lou was no stranger to evil and its tricky ways. Her eyes had taken the measure of many odd things. Yes, she'd dealt with plenty of evil in her life because she carried the Sight.

Neglect. The place had been abandoned. No hand had been turned to the work it needed in a long time. Everywhere she looked, there was work to be done. Weeds to pull so flowers could grow again. Dust to sweep away so life could begin again.

Things rustled and whispered as she shoved the door of the little cabin open. The door hinges shrieked in protest. *A little oil will do the trick there,* she thought. *As for the other noises, we'll see.*

She stepped just inside, sniffed the air and listened, then drew her conclusion. It was safe. *Just the scents of animals livin' out their lives,* she thought. *Nothin' more.* The cabin smelled stale but not evil. Not spellbound. *Nothin' bad lurkin' in here. The energy was benign.*

The cabin was bigger than it looked from outside, with one large room and what looked like another good size room to the back. Lou set her suitcase down beside the old couch in the living room before she crossed into the smaller room. Two rusty twin size bed frames with no mattresses stood side by side up against the back wall. Lou grinned.

Following her instincts, she'd carried three featherbeds with her to this place. Now she knew why. Pieces of the puzzle that had drawn her here were falling into place.

Lou took her time checking everything inside and out. The cabin held a good cook stove and a clean fireplace. There were a couple cords of fresh cut firewood stacked neatly against an outside wall. All her questions about who and why someone sent her here ebbed away as she settled in. Who cares? She was tired of traveling.

Lou cleaned off the old couch in the living room and flung her feather bed over it. She tossed the extra two featherbeds on the twin beds in the back room. The couch would do. She didn't like to sleep in beds any more. They reminded her of too much love lost, memories she avoided these days.

She was beyond tired. A long drive. But she'd made it. She wandered over to the couch, laid down. The old couch made a good bed. It was soft and lumpy in just the right places. She fell asleep.

She woke up at the crack of dawn to birds singing loudly and other animals making a racket. As soon as she sat up, the racket stopped. She lay back down and the noises started again. When she sat up again, the noises stopped. She got up and made coffee and went to work.

A short time later, she pitched a small tent close to a corner of the cabin porch. She made a fire pit and ringed it with stones a few steps to the right, away from the tent, farther out into the side yard. She laid an old refrigerator grill over the two level flat rocks on each side of the fire pit and settled the iron pot she used for cooking pinto beans long and slow onto the grill. It stayed level. That was good.

She set the pot for washing her clothes and sheets beside the fire pit. She cooked and washed clothes outside in summer to keep the heat out of the house. She planned to sleep in the tent on the nights when the moon was nowhere to be seen, and the house felt like it held her too close in the darkness.

Lou went out and tried to start her car. It was deader than a doornail. She'd figured as much. She strolled over to the rusted out old station wagon parked beside the house. She opened the driver's door. A key lay on the driver's seat. She got in and put the key in the ignition. The old rust bucket started right up. She sighed, relieved. Turned the ignition off. Pocketed the key. Climbed out of the old station wagon. Gave it a pat. Somebody was still looking out for her.

Lou was no fool. She was quick to catch on to the fact that the fun was just beginning in her new home. She tried to sleep past dawn the first few mornings, but the birds and other animals raised hell when she tried to let her arthritis ease just a little bit longer.

She was quick to figure out that something or somebody was in a hurry for her to get a bunch of work done around the cabin. Because of it, she was forced to drag her sorry ass out of the bed at the crack of dawn each morning and set to work.

I'm having to keep to somebody else's time schedule. Definitely not mine, she thought resentfully. *The Unseens were mostly just as hard on a body as the damn Seens were with their government rules!*

Lou drove the old station wagon into Gitwell, the nearest town, thirteen miles away. It didn't take her long to realize that she would get no help from its citizens.

The close mouthed, strange bunch living in Gitwell told her a few skimpy things as she shopped their stores. They told her the huge, dark house by her cabin was Manfred's Folly, named after Dolly Manfred's unpleasant, unfortunate, and very dead, weird, murdered family. Lou nodded. She had to drive by the Folly every time she went anywhere. She knew other words for that house's evil doings. A long past and still evil lived there.

The few old people left in Gitwell told her the cabin was once called Folly's Cottage. But cottage was too polite a word for the shacky, weathered little cabin built long ago out of leftovers from the Folly.

Nobody in Gitwell seemed to remember exactly when Manfred's Folly or Folly's Cottage were built. The tiny courthouse in Gitwell, population ninety-eight, burned down quite a while back; no one remembered quite when. The burning included most of the records of the town's citizenry and lands, including Dolly Manfred's Folly.

No proof of anything anywhere, Lou thought resentfully. She thought of the deed she'd received through the mail. It was safe in a metal box, buried under the huge tree in the cabin yard with a protector spinning above it.

Word was that the little burg of Gitwell was growing like crazy until Dolly Manfred and her bad bunch killed each other off in the fancy mansion next door to the cabin. Then Gitwell started dying off too. It was slowly losin' people and shrinking down into nothing. Only ninety-eight people left.

Lou shook her head dolefully as she drove out of Gitwell. Gitwell's residents were changing for the worse, and nobody in town realized what was going on. All hundred or so of them. *Well,* she thought grimly, *bad always turns to evil, and evil always takes an action if it is let loose of long enough. Trouble.*

When she tried to speed up going past Manfred's Folly, the old station wagon coughed and sputtered. Time to get it tuned up, she thought grimly. No way could she do without a good running vehicle.

She put the pedal to the medal. Nothing happened. The old station wagon lurched along at the same speed. *It seems it has two speeds. Slow and stop.* Lou thought grimly.

She drove into her driveway and came to a stop beside the dead car. *One dead and one slow.* She thought, getting out and slamming the car door shut. *Gonna' have to fix that problem.*

She stalked into the cabin. Grabbed a biscuit and broke it open. Poured a little honey in it and ate it as she walked the floor. *Too many evils to think about.* Then she took a long, well deserved nap.

In self-defense she walked her property over and over until she was clear exactly where the property lines were. Her new home needed to be separated from Manfred's Folly. It did not need to be a part of The Folly's history any longer. Or Gitwells.

The job would be hard and require a lot of work and time. But it had to be done.

But first things first. Lou got out her map and studied it. A few days later, she drove the old station wagon around Gitwell, not going through the middle of town, avoiding Main Street, following her map and instincts until she came to a stop in front of a car repair shop ninety miles away.

The faded, dusty board out front announced that the shop was Mr. Good Knight's Auto Repair. A tall man with gray hair and wise, wary eyes strolled out, wiping his hands on a rag. Silently, they looked each other over. Something flashed between them. In a couple minutes, they nodded at each other.

Lou sat still and waited in the driver's seat. Mr. Good Knight placed his hands on his hips and strolled leisurely around the station wagon, looking it over. Then he popped the hood, propped it up, and looked underneath. A lengthy time passed. He closed the hood and strolled back to the driver's window.

He peered in at Lou. "I'm Mr. Good Knight. You can call me Mr. You'll need what I call a super tune-up on this junk heap. Don't go washin' it. Just keep the winda's clean, so you can see where you're goin'."

She nodded, opened the door, and climbed out, handing him the keys.

"What's your name?"

"Ms. Louise Hope Cornfield," she answered. He studied her. She glared at him. Finally he said, "Ms. Cornfield. There's a place to stay right there."

He pointed at the small RV camp across the gravel road.

"You'll need this ride dolled up right away. An' it'll take me a day or two."

She nodded.

"It's gonna' take some bucks." he warned.

She shrugged. Serious cash had been included in the large envelope along with the deed.

"Don't do it up cheap."

Lou stayed at the RV camp until the station wagon was done. When she picked it up, Mr.

Good Knight said, "Bring her back in two weeks. Had to order a couple parts. But she's the fastest thing on the road now, and a couple other things, in disguise. Just don't wash her and blow her cover, okay? Rain won't hurt her, though," he answered her unspoken question. The car problem was taken care of.

It was time tackle the next problem. Lou drove to a town in the opposite direction of Gitwell. She stopped at their lumber yard and bought fencing supplies. A few thin, metal posts, plain pasture fencing. She fitted what she could into the station wagon and drove home. She wanted to hurry, but wasn't able to. She was too little and too old to do much at a time.

She put up the fencing, one post at a time, going as slow as she had to. The work took up most of her first summer on her new property. Finally, the yard was fenced. "No Trespassing" signs were posted. Any kind of Darkness looking to hurt somebody would know it was trespassing now.

Lou began her next project. It was time to make the gadgets that would bring protection to her new home. Gadgets that would disseminate bad energies. Her property needed protection from the evils emanating from Manfred's Folly.

Lou's Sight took over the job. It led the way, as usual. She'd made devices with Sight guiding her many times before. Algebra wasn't for fools like her. Maybe not for angels, either. Nor that cantankerous geometry. Forget that. She let her Sight bring each contrivance together naturally. She spread aluminum foil around here and there. She hung thingamajigs from the ceiling. Everything she made owned its own voice. Each one rattled or binged or tinged or banged or sang. Each one made some kind of noise for fun or when necessary. They worked hard, efficiently dissipating bad energies or giving off warning sounds of evil approaching.

Lou knew plenty about evil. Her life had started right off with Darkness. Dating clear back to her birth. She didn't remember how many years ago that was. But it was plenty.

She'd been thrown into the Light at birth. She was a second twin. Born to a mother screaming in astonishment at a second birth. A mother thinking she was dying instead of birthing. Aunt Nanny Brevity had scolded her mother. Ordered her mother to quit acting like she was dying, that she'd mark that second baby girl for life if she'd didn't stop being so foolish. Still, her mother screamed her way through Lou's birth and Aunt Nanny Brevity's prediction of a fearful life came true. Auntie named her Louise Hope. Lou's childish mother had turned to her twin and left Lou to make her own way in the world.

Lou fought for her life, alone. But the Darkness gifted her with a companion. You know, to keep her company the rest of her life.

Mr. Fear was Darkness's number one gift to her. A faithful companion, Lou and Mr. Fear became well acquainted. For all of her young life, Mr. Fear showed up whenever he damn well pleased. Which was most every day of her life. Growing up, Lou couldn't predict her reaction to anything. She'd trembled like a plucked violin string most of her life, organs roaring, mind hiding, while Mr. Fear terrorized her soul, driving her heart into triple beats, her adrenals into racing.

She'd lived in pure, exhausting hell until the day she went to the library and came across a book about the concept, the art of disassociation, dissemination, and to put it plainly, splitting herself apart into useful pieces.

Better than un-useful pieces, she'd thought grimly. She grabbed the book, sat down and swiftly read the book all the way through. She stole the book. It became her Bible.

She realized she was the perfect candidate for the techniques in the book. By the time she was fourteen, she could quickly and skillfully split herself into different parts that could handle whatever was going on. Mr. Fear was forced to take a backseat. But he remained waiting in the wings. And she knew it.

About that time, her Sight held a come to Jesus meeting with her. Her Sight informed her that in order to keep Mr. Fear waiting in the wings instead of onstage, she had to do something. Become a Heroine of some kind...

Lou gave up and gave in. She tried but couldn't find out who she inherited the Sight from in her family. She didn't know if having Sight was a curse or a blessing. Her family was convinced Sight was a curse.

Sometimes she wanted to go kick somebody's ass over her "gift". Nobody else in her bunch could see "unseens", so they shunned her. They couldn't see sensible stuff about life, either. They said she was crazy. Nuts. Well, she liked her backwards bunch just about as much as they liked her!

Lou stayed alone and lonely. No plan for her future. Her Sight took the lead. Lou let it. Soon her Sight discovered a church Lou could serve in as a healer. A sanctuary. At last. The church became her home, its people her family. It wasn't long before Lou became a missionary and went on the road. She became a "roadie for sweet baby Jesus." Lou was a Heroine to all the church people. Over the years, she became legendary for her fights against evil.

Lou Cornfield, roadie for sweet baby Jesus, drove the rusty old buckets people donated to her all over the country, stopping in little backwoods places, healing and advising people. Then moving on, before things got too hot. For there were those who lived in support of evil.

People who didn't like it taken down. To them, she was a curse.

Her Sight grew stronger, driving her from town to town while honing its abilities. When she felt sorry for herself, lonely or homeless, her Sight ordered her to get her sorry ass on the move and get on with her job of fighting evil. She was good at her work. She knew when to stay and when to leave. She'd been called out to do all kinds of jobs for the Good Lord because of her Sight. She left quickly before being noticed from each place, each job well done.

Yep. So there came a time when Mr. Fear didn't come around very often any more. Just in deep, unexpected pockets, making her heart flutter and her breathing fast, using up precious time. But it was quickly over and she went her way.

She never backed down from the fight against the darkness of Evil. She'd changed names and parts of herself plenty of times to keep herself safe from retaliation, so she could go on doing the Sighted work needed for sweet baby Jesus. She had changed hair color. Clothes. Living here and there and anywhere. Whatever it took, so folks who had the Sighted Good could keep on working to spite the evil doings in this old world.

Her Sight had made a homespun healer of her, and given her a family and a root home to come back to. But mostly she was a lonely missionary. That was okay with her. Most of the time. The rest of the time she yearned for a man and a different life.

Years passed. She wore herself out. Grew tired. Exhausted, Lou began to crave a home of her own. A place where she could live out the rest of her life. For the first time, she yearned to put down roots. Get off the road. She yearned for a place to rest. A peaceful place. Ground to walk on that belonged just to her.

Her work for sweet baby Jesus had gone well over the years, but she was worn out. She didn't have enough energy to heal anyone else in her old age anymore without pulling it from herself, and she needed all the energy she had to live.
She waited for a sign.
Jesus on the main line-call me up sometime.
But He didn't.

She waited and waited for sweet baby Jesus to show her the way, but it didn't happen. Finally, she gave up and settled on a new plan. She'd go out the way she came in. Scared almost to death's door, alone. Oh, yeah.

She lived alone and thrifty, running out of money, living in a cheap little motel room in a little burg until the note, the bundle of cash, and the legal looking deed arrived in a large, official envelope with no stamps on it. Somebody had placed it in her mailbox by hand.

Those three things, the note, the deed, and the money, set Lou free. She packed up and left for Colorado in a matter of minutes.

Well, now she'd made it to this cabin and into her old age, hoping her Work for Good was ending. She hoped to rest easy in her old age. Missionary-ing was over.

Lou stopped hoeing her garden and studied her place. One small outbuilding that once housed a horse. Now it housed Bessie the cow and Louella and Lenny, the two chickens. She let them run in the front yard where the land emanated good energies.

Her eyes wandered over dandelions and hepatica. They were still bloomin'. Those two toughies lasted longest in this high, dry climate.

An old outhouse stood in the far corner of the yard. She kept it freshly limed. Its weathered boards were almost covered by flowering bushes on both sides and the back. *Poo's one of the best fertilizer sources God ever made,* she thought, grinning. *Plenty of that around!*

No dogs. No cats. Just Bessie the cow grazin' down the grass each day under the old, wide, tall trees to the Good workin' side of the house. No animals allowed on the place except for the two fat, contented chickens, Louella and Lennie. Louella and Lennie stayed near Bessie. Bessie just wanted to graze and be petted and milked. She liked tending her animals and her garden. She was leading a simple and good life. So far.

She eyed her yard. It was packed full of yard decorations, made per her Sight's orders. Lou had placed the first protection devices-yard decorations-along the survey flags and around the cabin. She positioned shields and evil catching inventions wherever her instincts led her. Her Sight was the big boss of that project. It knew what needed doing.

Lou's supernatural protection inventory was still growing. She'd placed the latest instruments she'd made on the edge of the flat field between her place and Manfred's Folly. There were a lot of protectors gathered there now, and she was making more.

The new devices would redirect the energies emanating from the big ugly Folly, creating an interruption in the view. The protectors would limit what the negative energies could see, hiding the cabin from their view. For she knew well that Evil has Sight, too.

Lou hoped the contrivances worked to their fullest capacity. She had nailed the Good Lord's crosses and rusty tin cans with nail holes punched in the bottom of 'em on stakes all over the yard. They would grab the smaller, bad, wanderin' wisps that drifted near her place from the Folly.

Other contraptions were there to warn her. Some trapped swooney ghosts, mean little things that swooped about day or night tryin' to depress people into havin' a weak soul. They also trapped pommies, the little round electric things trying to get into a person and electrocute em' real slow. Spirals staved them off, creating a maze that caused them to get lost. Hee hee.

The tin cans caught bad things and tossed them up so the air could grab 'em and banish 'em away. Spirit Catchers. Mobiles. They swung in the wind, chatterin' like hell when anything on the place moved a hair. They were the best tattle tales she could think of. Why, they owned the place in some ways. Sing your songs sweet catcher plans.

Lou grinned. She stood up and stretched her back while she studied the lace curtains over the windows in the cabin. Their patterns were designed to turn away curiosity. Granny Parse's man had sewn them together out of scraps from Granny's sewing materials.

The odd-shaped lace pieces in the faded curtains slanted in every direction a person or thing could think of, making anyone or anything nosing around un-curious and not giving a damn about what lay behind the curtains. She narrowed her eyes and studied the patterns on the curtains. Lou had hung those curtains up over many windows these many years. Now they covered the windows of her cabin.

Lou cast weary, shrewd thoughts that had taken the measure of many unseen, strange things in her life to the other side of her cabin. She stayed away from there. She couldn't see them, but she knew the pale blue foxglove bloomed in great, tall spikes, righteously deadly and beautiful over there. The foxglove bloomed tall in the summer and low and purposeful in the winter, keeping steadfast vigilance. Poking up short and impatient through the snow and ice and wind, waiting for the power evil gives off.

Waiting patiently with their cold, delicate magnetic touch to suck that power in, poison it, and shoot it back out in a concentrated, unseen energy stream back to its evil source, causing that source to slowly fade away from the poison.

The foxglove seeds had been a gift from Granny Parse, given to Granny way back when Cumberland Gap was still filled with the dog eared Elementals from their bogs and Big eared things ruling the Old Mountains. The Elemental Beings living back there now, kept to themselves and shunned those who might make the mistake of thinking they were harmless.

I'll be gone 'fore you ever use 'em, so jist' remember to keep yourself away from ever' single one of 'em. Mind me, hear?

Lou kept the seed packet for years before it came time to use them. She had buried the seeds in fresh dug soil at that side of the cabin before she'd slept her first night on her new property.

She planted the seeds just as Granny Parse had long ago instructed. They went in the ground quick when she discovered Mandfred's Folly squatting like an ugly toad next door to her new home.

The foxglove and many odd, beautiful blooms and vines grew up almost overnight under the shade trees and bushes on that side of the cabin, all of their faces pointed towards Manfred's Folly, watching, waiting. They kept to their side of the cabin. Lou stayed away from that side of the cabin, for she knew they would have to hurt her too, if she got in their way. Lou heeded Granny Parse's words of warning. What they did was none of her business. They had their own life and ways to tend to.

I've been here almost three years. Lou thought. She went back to hoeing her garden, tossing potato pieces into the too-deep v's she'd dug in the garden rows. As she worked, she contemplated the name she went by these days. How she got this name, she didn't remember. Probably one of those higher up bossy Sight unseens that ran her life, had stuck her with the name.

Her high nerves had caused her to dig too deep, too quick on some of the Vs waiting in the ground to hug the potato eyes. She knew from past experience that the spuds would never come up if she buried them too deep. Impatiently, she kicked dirt back into a few of the holes with a worn sneaker before she tossed the spud quarters in and covered them with dirt.

Louise Hope Cornfield. It was a corny name. She snickered. It sure as hell wasn't the name she'd started out life with!

Well, she'd ended up living on this mountain. She'd learned the ropes the last couple of years and made things work. She liked some things about this place. Some things she didn't. She liked the heavy snow and the howling winds trying to find ways to get into her snug little cabin in the winter. She'd patched it up and laughed at the wind. Summer wasn't so bad, either. Dry and high, it was here. Now it was spring again. Her second or third year on this place. But the good times wouldn't last much longer. Something bad was going to happen. Soon. Very soon. No more weeks left. Just days. Time was closing in on her. She could feel it.

Lou looked up from her work, startled, fearful. Something in back of the flat field that ran behind Manfred's Folly had moved. Back of the field loomed a dark forest that seemed to move here and there as it pleased. Lou grimaced in fear. That black, shadowy forest was a supernatural Dreadful Forest. She wasn't about to get nosy about any of its workings! She went back to work.

After awhile, Lou decided to take a break. Drank some water from the canning jar nestled in an old hollow tree root at the end of the garden.

Squinting small, deep-set eyes, she examined her small, old-fashioned cabin. It was the only other place on the dusty little excuse for a road running past Manfred's Folly.

She needed to get more chickens later, if she was still alive after the fight against evil was over. More chickens would raise babies and lay good eating eggs. Chickens didn't care about anything except their own housekeeping. But those old hens made for golden fried chicken and buttery mashed taters from the garden on Sunday afternoons.

Wind soughed through the three tall pine trees that lined the front of the house. Some of their branches swept the ground. Other branches rode high in the air. The pines kept most of her tiny place hid from the view of the road. God knows what all the pine trees must have seen with all their veins and leaves and all they wove.

The time was drawing near. Well, so be it. There was plenty of stuff around to help her ward off the small evils for a little while longer. But it wasn't enough, and she knew it.

Dere's hells bells ringin'
hidin' in a silly lookin' maze
but don't kid yo'self
ever one in dere'
is got dere' own ways
a' takin' care of bidness'.

Chapter Two

Lou Cornfield's cabin set beside the thin, dusty, dead-end lane that ran past Manfred's Folly, her cabin, twisted through vacant land, and ended. When she needed to, she drove into Gitwell to take care of business. She kept her eyes fixed straight ahead when she drove past Manfred's Folly, not looking right or left. She kept the pedal to the metal like she was a NASCAR driver in a race, flying past the ugly old mansion and the dark forest lurking behind the flat field.

It helped that no one suspected that there was a mojo, hard-assed, speed master engine hidden under the hood of the rusty old station wagon.

After more of those whatever they were-bad!-things had moved into The Folly awhile back, the county had put up a Dead End sign just past her cabin.

The county supposedly put the sign up to discourage people from driving down the thin, dusty lane running past Manfred's Folly. They said they were afraid someone might torch the old Folly. First the dead end sign, then they placed a trespassing sign in front of The Folly. Lou guessed that the Gitwell folks and their kin didn't want anyone nosing around.

Now, only the mailman and delivery people traveled the lane past The Folly to her place. The Dead End sign had been up six weeks. Nobody came down the road to check on it any more. Well, they could do as they pleased, but Lou had a plan of her own.

Early one morning, she built up the campfire. But she wasn't washing clothes today. The fire was for something else. After the fire was roaring, she snuck her small chain saw out of the cabin and hurried down the road. Quickly she cut the post the "Dead-End" sign was nailed on in two pieces. She hurried the pieces of the wood post back to the campfire by the porch and tossed them in the fire, and went back for the sign. She cut the screaming, harsh yellow metal sign with its glaring black painted letters into sixteen pieces, gathered up the pieces, and buried them deep in the ground across the road from where they had been.

She buried them flat side down in a long row, then cleaned up the spot where the Dead End sign once stood until it looked so natural, nobody would ever know a sign had ever been erected there.

While she worked, Lou thought grimly, *There isn't gonna' be any dead-end anything around my home! Hope abounded. Hope was the name of the game. And it was her middle name. Louise Hope Cornfield. Puddin' and 'tane. Ask her agin' an' she'd tell you the same. Yes. Hope lived strong in her. Not for the past. For the future. Keep goin' ahead! was her motto.*

When she was done, it was still early. She watched the sun rise while she sipped hot coffee and ate a biscuit with honey by the fire. Now there just the mailman and delivery people who used the lane to get to her cabin. She'd put a stop to that, too.

She rented a mailbox at the post office in Stemmons, a little town thirty miles away to make sure there weren't any packages or mail for nosy Herman the Gitwell mailman or anyone else to deliver.

When she was done, Miss Louise Hope Cornfield drove into Gitwell. She visited in town, making out like she was infirm and couldn't remember crap. That she was just an old woman living in a tiny cottage, mindin' her own business, an old woman with a little memory trouble from old age. She'd die alone of old age all by herself when the Good Lord said it was time, she told people. They bought her act, and didn't bother with her. All was well. Her bases were covered.

All that was left was Manfred's Folly to focus on. A batch of new people had moved in recently. Lou had slipped out back and hunkered down, hiding, watching the stream of beat-up hippie campers, junk cars, and rusty vans driving in, music blasting, parking in the field behind The Folly.

Sometimes the new people held gatherings out back of The Folly. On those nights, the air thickened with bad things. Miss Louise Hope Cornfield kept her sorry ass cooped up inside her cottage on those nights. The curtains swayed, working hard, pushing away the bad energies. She walked the floor. No sleep on those nights.

One morning, after one of their filthy night gatherings, Lou went out to her garden. Something had walked her corn patch the night before and flattened a path through it. A watermelon lay just past it, crushed to itty pieces like somebody or something had tossed it into a chopper with big jaws. It lay in pieces at the end of a corn row.

She looked further. Protection devices were on tilt. Others lay in pieces on the ground. Others were okay. Still working. She went back in the cabin and got a basket. Gathered up the shattered parts. Mourned over their twisted, broken shapes.

She took them to the porch and set the basket down. Then she went back to the garden. *There was still an evil there to address.* She shuddered and began chanting prayers. She hurried to the small shed and grabbed a shovel. She shoveled up the mess on the ground and the dirt under the mess, careful to not touch the filth of it.

She carried the filth to the burn barrel and threw it in. She made five trips before it was all in the burn barrel. She struck a match and threw it in the burn barrel. Stinking, hot, enraged foul air blasted out. Lou jumped out of the way and prayed hard to sweet Baby Jesus until the fire started to burn clean again.

Yes. The evil was growing bolder. Taking its time. Stalking its prey. Growing stronger in that nasty old house.

The bad energies made Lou's bones ache that night and she dreamed Shadow dreams. The dreams warned her that the evil was closing in on her. The dreams told her the time of Reckoning was coming soon. Beware and prepare!

Lou had been involved in a few Reckonings before, and she was terrified of them. Some folks called them Come to Jesus Meetings. Others called them Come to Satan Meetings. She didn't want to be involved in either one.

Lou's nerves grew short. She had to have help. When was help going to arrive? Did the big bosses who ran her Sighted show really expect her to handle the evil in thay nasty old Manfred's Folly all by herself? No way!

She'd gone to bed every night, praying for somebody to come quick and help her. No answer. She grew desperate. In only the most desperate of circumstances did she ask Sister Moaner for help.

Sister Moaner just happened to be a Wraith. She saw to it that Lou stayed fresh for every battle with evil by getting enough sleep. Sister Moaner moaned and wailed Lou into a drugged sleep when a battle with evil was portending, so she'd at least get some rest before the battle.

But Sister Moaner was prone to traveling. Prone to not staying in touch. Prone to being busy counting the constellations in stone walls centuries old when she was needed elsewhere. Sister Moaner heard Lou and finally showed up. They moaned together all night long.

No rest for the wicked or the innocent, either! Lou thought the next morning, dragging herself out of bed to make a pot of black, strong coffee. When it was ready, she drank it hot, heavily sugared, plenty of milk. When she was done, she neatened her long hair into a braid, pinned it up, and changed clothes. Then she set to work on another cross.

Well, today is today, she thought. *Let the past be done for now.* She gave up ruminating over all the history that had happened before this day.

She thought, *Yep. I'm an escape artist. But I ain't runnin' away this time. Not when the job is done. I'm staying put.*

She thought about the property just past her place and on down the lane. It was Good. Filled with clean energies, waiting for something. If worst came to worse, she'd haul herself down and hide on that nice piece of vacant property up around the bend from her place. That ground held pretty pine trees and good soil. Somebody had come out recently and made a small trail across it, and surveyed it.

She'd walked down that way and examined the small red and yellow flags outlining the property. She liked to walk that land. Made her feel stronger. Maybe because that land was never lived on. Well, somebody was coming to roost there a spell.

A little later she thought, *Well, company's comin'. Gonna' have to fry up some chicken and make biscuits.* The next morning, after hot coffee and a bit of contemplation, she fired up the old rusty station wagon and got in. Absent minded, she sat still a minute. She touched her white hair with a callused finger. She bleached it white when it needed it. Her roots grew in dark brown instead of white. Her mother's hair did the same thing. Not one gray hair the day she died. Smooth skin. No wrinkles. Lou felt old. And needed to look old. But people wouldn't think so if her hair was brown. She was feeling better.

Some of her trepidation was gone. She turned the key in the ignition and headed into Gitwell to pick up her company.

This place was just what she needed, she thought, *even though it made her a little bit breathless to think of living so high up in the mountains, she wasn't about to give up the cabin. It was hers. She'd keep it, and pay whatever price was required.*

Headin' down to Hope town
the sun shinin' in my shoes
still lookin' for' a place
where I can toss my blues

Chapter Three

Shem Rickleman

Shem Rickleman, hobo, was plumb wore out. He'd been on the road too damn long. Not much luck hitchhiking this time. He needed to find a hiding place and rest for awhile. His wiry, five-and-a-half-foot tall frame was bent forward under the weight of his backpack. He made himself out to be a hiker, a moneyed, and therefore, carefree young man just walking to see the world, taking a sabbatical away from school. At first he'd been in junior college, then in college. Now, at his age, he was a wandering teacher or a professor.

Shem's hair, once light blond, had darkened to a medium brown over the years. Wild and thick, sticking up in wiry, tough coils, it grew like wildfire. He kept it cut short, but it grew back fast. *It seems like it grows back overnight,* he thought, ruefully rubbing a wide, stubby hand over his burr head.

Shem was thinking about people. They were weird. They'd give him money for school, eagerly shoving it at him, but not if he told them the truth.

That he'd been on the road most of his life. That his was a sketchy sixth grade education. That his parents dumped him out on the world when he was twelve, and there was nobody to take him in. That he'd survived and learned street smarts and wised up after learning some very painful lessons.

The scared boy he once was, had begged his grandparents to take him in, but his old sonofabitch grandfather wouldn't take do it. Well, in the long run, that had turned out to be a good thing. At the state school, he'd learned discipline for the first time in his life. He'd been working on that ever since.

If he'd stayed with his grandparents when he was a kid, he would have ended up a career criminal, like his uncles. The discipline he learned at the state school kept him alive on the streets when somebody bigger than him—and most men were—tried to beat him or abuse him in more personal ways.

He wasn't running from the law, just from himself and searching to find his mother. Shem was twelve when his mother ran away from home. From his father. Shem was too young to be on his own. But the best thing his mother ever did for him was to give him the gift of truth about his father before she ran.

She told him that the man she was running away from was not Shem's biological father. Shem felt nothing except a vast relief at her words. The rutting, low life animal with the IQ of a randy billy goat who claimed to be his father was not his biological father! It was the best news of his life. Shem's mother said his real father was French, from Louisiana and his name was on Shem's birth certificate and that they got together because they both loved hot air balloons and he'd taken her up in his little two seater plane. But they'd lost each other. She didn't have time to tell him more before she left. She had told him his real father's name! Her words set him free to begin a new life.

When Shem got out of the state school, he applied for his birth certificate and changed his last name to his father's real name. He tried to look him up, but couldn't find him. Then he looked up his three younger half-brothers. They were all gone. Either dead or adopted out somewhere.

Shem moved on. When he longed for family, he reminded himself that his other half-siblings were just like their father and would no doubt stay that way. The apples wouldn't fall far from that tree. He'd seen that before his mother deserted them. He didn't know where they were.

In Heaven, Hell, or maybe still on Earth. He didn't care to exert himself to find them.

But his mother. That was different. A young, willowy blond with sky blue eyes. The eyes of an angel. A full mouth that laughed widely at her world. She'd kissed his cheeks dozens of times holding his face with her thin, long pale hands. She had to be somewhere hiding out in this old world. He would find her someday and take care of her. And she'd hold his face and hug him once again. Shem knew he would stay unsettled and on the road until he found her.

The years had passed swiftly. Shem was approaching thirty. Lately, he'd begun to yearn for a place of his own. A place he wouldn't have to leave. A home. He was getting awfully tired of being on the road.

He was no longer the boy who had settled his thinking about his family and moved on years ago. The boy that left family behind to become a homeless transient, living any place but where the people who'd rejected him lived. He was now one of those people who laughed silently inside himself whenever someone pitied him for being on the road, for he liked this new life much better than his old one.

Besides, he knew his mother's family well enough to know he'd inherited some form of Sight from them. That Sight warned him away from bad things. Protected him. Gave him information. His Sight came in handy quite a few times, especially at the start of being on his own, until he got the lay of the land.

Shem had seen the ugly, been hurt but not bent by it, and ran from it. He escaped successfully each time. He was an Escape Artist, a Walker, walking the world with no place to stop yet, he sometimes told himself with a wide mouth, full-lipped grin before his smile faded at the horrors he'd survived.

For some reason, he'd landed in Colorado this time, in a part of the state and in a little town he didn't like. And he went by his feelings whenever he needed to change course. *It was a matter of seeing what was in front of a person,* he thought. It was just Sight. Common sense. No big deal.

Shem spent the night behind the grocery store, hidden beneath bushes at the back of the parking lot.

He woke up early. The grocery store would open early. The western store opened late. He knew from past experience that bars had lots of comings and goings through back doors. Grocery stores did too. Grocery deliveries. Clothing stores...not much. Barbershops...not much. But he couldn't afford to go inside those.

He took out his small rectangle of mirror and a pair of small scissors, and quickly trimmed his hair. He was an old hand at this job. He couldn't afford to look too wild and wooly.

Hairy was acceptable if he was clean shaven and neat. He needed to keep on it because his hair grew faster than anyone could imagine. If he didn't, it would be sticking out around his head like a wild bramble bush in no time. He dry-shaved his heavy beard next. He grinned at himself in the mirror and put his shaving kit away.

The kids in state school nicknamed him craggy werewolf because of his face and hair. Maybe he sprang from a wooly ancestor, he thought. He grinned his wide grin and patted the short, sharp knife he carried in a sheath under his shirt.

Seems like he'd at least got a sense of humor from whoever he sprung from. His mother had run away from who he once believed was his father, worn out from his constant, never-ending, never holding down a job, insistently rutting on top of her and eating mindlessly like an animal while she cooked. Shem pushed away the memories.

Clean-shaven and presentable for the day, he packed up and headed for the grocery store. That's when his Sight turned him towards the old woman trying to lift too many groceries at one time into her ratty old station wagon.

He strolled over to help her. The closer he got, the more his heart pounded. By the time he reached her, he felt winded, like he'd run a hard three miles or more. His Sight was telling him something, but he didn't have a clue what it was. He just knew he had to meet this old woman who was somehow in disguise.

The old woman watched him approach with shrewd eyes. He reached her and stopped. He stared into eyes as old as the Earth's first rain and young as the lone dandelion blooming in the dust by the cracked gray sidewalk at feet.

"Git' in the backseat," the old woman ordered him in a low voice, tossing the grocery sacks in the back of the station wagon like they weighed little to nothing.

Shem froze.

The old woman frowned.

"Git' in and lay down 'fore they see's ya."

He studied the creases and lines on her face for a split second, maybe it was an eternity. The lines led to routes he'd never taken before, but wanted to as a Walker, forever.

"Okay."

Shem got in and hunkered down. Disappeared. The woman closed the back door, strolled around, and climbed into the front seat of the old rust bucket. He heard the engine turn over like it was new. It purred instead of rattled.

He started to sit up. She said, "Stay down until we git' home. I don't want 'em to see ya' when we go by their root place."

Root place? Shem had no idea what she meant. He shut up and hunkered down. Lou drove past Manfred's Folly and parked beneath the trees at the side of her cabin. Shem sat up and looked around.

He got out, turned in a circle, and let out a low whistle. Before he could say anything, she said, "Don't touch ary' one of them flares' or bushes, vines...Don't touch nothin' ...help me git' these supplies into the house."

Shem obediently grabbed up grocery bags and followed the old woman inside. She thumped the bags down on the table, turned around, and pointed toward the back room.

"Your'n is that room there. I cleared it out last night. You'll jist' hafta' put up with the stuff in there. I don't want it touched or moved."

He nodded. He'd been around some strange people before. He didn't bother looking at the back room. If she was trying to kidnap him, she'd made a big mistake. He was bigger and stronger than she was.

"Anyone else living here?" Shem asked, eyes searching everywhere.

"Nope. Just us now. Me. Before. Alone."

He stared at her.

"You knew I was coming?"

"Yep. But not til' yestiddy, late. It would have been better if I'd a' had more time," she said resentfully. "Now we'll jist' hafta' make do. Sort things out as we go along."

"What do you mean?" Shem asked carefully, ready to sprint for the door.

She turned and looked at him.

"We got a hell of a big job on our hands to do. Come on."

She stepped out on the porch and waited. Shem took off his backpack and set it down. Then he followed her to the porch, down the steps and around the side of the house, ducking and whistling involuntarily at all the crosses, mobiles, and other contraptions sticking up out of the ground.

The old woman led him around the side of the house and back to her garden. Shem was kept busy watching his feet while trying to keep from touching the odd objects in his path.

The old woman stopped and pointed her finger at something. Shem stopped, looked up, and saw The Folly. A searing flash of pain hit his third eye. He fell backward and landed on his rump in the soft garden dirt. He sat up, staring at the monstrosity towering over them like a giant dark boogeyman.

Shem knew plenty about distances. About miles. He measured the distance between them with his eyes. *Only a couple city blocks away,* he thought in dismay. *Much too close for comfort. Another state, another planet, would have been far better.*

"Better pay more attention to what you're doing." the old woman scolded him. "Better not get caught off guard like that again. That there thing is called The Folly or Manfred's Folly. It was Dolly Manfred's home place. My name is Lou. Louise Hope Cornfield. What's yours?"

"Shem," he answered. He hesitated on his last name.

"Don't bother," Lou said. I don't need to know. I got cold fried chicken in the fridge. And biscuits. Made 'em last night. I'll tell you about things while we eat."

The cold, crisp fried chicken was the best he'd ever tasted. They ate it with biscuits and a skillet of fried taters and drank buttermilk. Then they cleaned everything up and went to the front porch. Shem couldn't keep his eyes open.

Lou said, "Go get in your bed back there. We'll talk later."

Shem stood up and stumbled into the house and into the little back room. He noticed that there were two twin size beds, but he was to sleepy to ponder what that meant. He fell onto a featherbed and was asleep instantly.

Lou went back in the house a short time later. She crossed to a curtain strung on a wire in the corner of the room and pulled it shut. She'd hauled the old sofa behind it and set it just right.

"I believe I'll take a little nap, too."

Before she fell asleep she muttered, "Well, there's more people gets involved in these kinds of things than you'd ever think."

Dis' might be a damn good day
to think about runnin' away
from them big damn waves
of blue trouble that won't re-route

Chapter Four

Lily Jean Bloome and William the Dude

The sun shone warmth and lemon rays on everything around them. The ocean shaded into turquoise and blues, calmly rolling in and out in rhythmic, white edged rolls, leaving negative ions filtering through the air.

William the Dude and Lily Jean Bloome, housemates and sweethearts, were stretched out in lounge chairs on the beach behind her beach house. Barefoot and totally relaxed, they both wore rolled-up jeans and William's "official" white office shirts with long tails and rolled-up sleeves. On their heads were floppy white straw hats with "Fun in the Sun!' written in black script across the front.

They lay in their deck chairs, content, silent, staring out at the ocean for a long time. Then William said, "Can't take the sun like I used to."

Lily Jean Bloome didn't turn her head to take his measure as she usually did. Sadness mingled with resignation in her voice, she answered him. "Me neither." They both sighed.

After a long silence, William the Dude, mild mannered old prospector, former cattle rancher, and philosopher of Dudeism, spoke again.

"Back to Timmon." he said.

Lily Jean Bloome didn't answer.

He glanced sideways at the tall, big boned, beautiful, dignified woman sitting in the chair beside him. She was profound, intense, gentle and deep enough to carry her full name. He knew he was lucky he'd found her.

"Well, my dear Lily Jean Bloome, I think it's a good idea."

"I don't know, William," Lily Jean Bloome answered uneasily.

'Well, I don't see any other way of pulling him out of it. It's been a damn long year, and he's still depressed and useless."

"That's true," Lily Jean Bloome protested, "but that's where SHE is." She shivered.

William reached out to place a protective arm around her. Another long silence passed between them.

"I believe he's got to deal with her again before he can get on with his life. Hopefully, he's grieved enough and learned enough from Gordon to handle her hate and evil ways now." William said.

"Maybe. I still think it's too risky," she answered.

"Well, the deed is done. The letter is on its way to Gordon's."

Lily Jean Bloome turned to stare at him.

"I mailed it when you were in Los Angeles a couple days ago." He spoke mildly to offset her anger.

"Oh. I see," she mulled the information over, struggling and finally giving up her need to scold him. The deed was already done. Maybe it was for the best.

"Did you tell him SHE was there?"

"Nope. Just sent him a deed to some special property up the road from her."

"How is the property special?"

"It's got certain minerals on it. Rose quartz is layered through the soil, and it has the only gold laced peridot to be found north of a couple places in Texas. That combination makes it a protected place for him. Sort of sacred. Cowboy Johnson always said the Desert Store was centered on a healing chakra. Those are holy spots on the Earth where Good emanates from. I believe Timmons property in Colorado is one of them."

He looked away. He was always embarrassed about his own spirituality, his own intensity about life. She studied William with her usual curious affection.

"I've been too ambivalent about this, haven't I?"

"Maybe," William said. "Who knows? You know I wouldn't do anything to hurt him. He's a son to me, just as Avery Mott Judson was my brother, and Mama, my younger sister."

"Let's go visit Emma when this is over. She's got a show at an important gallery in New York in late summer," Lily Jean Bloome said impulsively, linking her arm through his.

"Well, okay. I'd love to see my daughter-and Alexander. It's been awhile. But let's see how this situation plays out first. It may take a while. Who knows how long we will have to stay on call?"

William patted her arm.

"I suspect it may be a long time."

Lily Jean Bloome sighed, laid her head on William the Dudes shoulder and they stared out to sea again.

Gordon

GRS or G.R.E.A.T.I.S., as his students called him, was a Master teacher of many magic skills. A teacher and a trainer of the Sighted Good, he thoroughly enjoyed training students and sending them off to their various posts to accomplish their work in a much more polished, skilled, and proper way when their training with him ended.

Gordon Tappenhouse Smythe owned many accomplishments. For one thing, he was a

Ranked Master in his realm of expertise in fighting evil.

Gordon stood six foot tall. Slim in a classic, fashionable 50's movie star way, he resembled Cary Grant, his favorite movie star even more, now that he was in his late sixties. Thick white hair, high cheekbones, able to wear a gunny sack and look handsome in it, women of all ages swooned over him. He'd adopted Cary Grant's refined movie mannerisms and his personal likes and dislikes.

Women swarmed after him just like they once did with Cary. Gordon had dated many and mated with a few, but none stuck. For behind his Cary Grant façade beat the heart of a true Master Mime, a soul with a cause and a purpose to fulfill. He was here to eradicate evil. No woman or child ever stood in the way of his life's mission. He'd been born to be on the stage, to train his own audience, to expand the use of their gifts through the many methods of suggestion and magic instead of boring, lengthy verbal explanations, which often ended in the failure of their missions.

Yes, Gordon Tappenhouse Smythe was also a Master Mime of great distinction. Mime was hid forte. The rock he stood upon when teaching.

He trained his students to dress properly for each occasion. He taught them social skills. He posed in his impeccably tailored clothes, displaying his impeccable manners in dining and social chit-chat via the Cary Grant method. His students paid attention and learned. If they didn't, he kicked them out.

Gordon's students adored him. He heard their reverent whispers and reveled in their awe, for he would never father children. He didn't want to. His students were his children. His position required his distinctive bachelorhood. He was grateful when his hormones had died down to a dull roar that allowed him to cultivate a distant, elegant intelligence that never strayed into moments of heated coupling again.

He made his students aware of their particular gifts and who they were in relationship to them through his tutoring. Their personalities were no accident, he told them. His wasn't either. He taught them how to wordlessly overcome almost any situation through the many forms of Mime, including perfecting the timing of shrugs, glances, murmurs, and posturing. No verbiage allowed. The problem had to be solved without it.

It was surprising to his students, but not to Gordon, how quickly they learned. He expected it.

When they began enjoying their newfound confidence too much, strutting around like proud peacocks, Gordon deliberately took them down a peg or two or more by taking them deeper into divination.

A Personal Philosophy was first gained, then embedded using his methods. When he finished training each student, they were dignified, philosophical steel magnets sheathed in cautious, competent magic; they were purposeful velvet, with great smiles, fantasy clothing, and the skills of a magician.

His highly trained and newly skilled students left his magic training lair infinitely more capable of accomplishing their missions using finesse, elegance, maturity, and discreet magic. The rest was in their hands.

Gordon had been content for a long time. But now there was a problem, and, it was turning out to be a very long term problem. The problem's name was Timmon.

Gordon and Timmon had met at a weekend house party. Gordon loathed certain social obligations he was forced to keep. The gathering they met at was one of them. Gordon noticed Timmon immediately upon his arrival. Noting Timmon's golden hair, blue eyes and angelic demeanor, Gordon thought smugly, *Another daddy's golden boy.* and turned away.

Then he heard Esme Stinton's sugar-sweet voice and turned back around to track it. Esme was one evil bitch, but hardly anyone ever guessed it, she hid her evil intentions so well. Only a few knew she'd got away with murder, and planned much more. The few that knew she was a monster, included him.

Gordon studied Esme warily. He efficiently avoided any confrontation with her, for she was not his to deal with. She knew this, and ignored him as though he didn't exist.

Esme looked angelic and completely innocent as usual in a baby blue sheath, her blond hair upswept, held in place with elegant combs.

She reached Timmon just as Gordon turned around. In amazement, he watched Esme reach out a hand and place it on Timmon's arm.

Timmon looked down at Esme with no expression. But Gordon saw the fire flash in his blue eyes. Unfortunately, Esme didn't notice Timmon's reaction to her. She expected the new boy on the block to respond like ones with no Sight always did.

But Timmon glared down at Esme with piercing eyes that told her he knew exactly what she was. Gordon watched as Esme finally realized that he saw through her. She recoiled and hurried away.

Well, maybe there was some entertainment here tonight, after all, Gordon thought.

He strolled over to Timmon, who'd taken up an uneasy stance near the entryway.

"Don't worry," he said easily to Timmon. "There are at least ten doors that I know of to escape from this room."

"I'm Gordon..." he waved his hand. "That will suffice."

He grinned at Timmon.

"How about a drink on the terrace?"

That was how they met. Gordon began training Timmon. Timmon trained Gordon in other things in return. All went well. Gordon and Timmon played their parts as student or teacher as needed with Gordon's other students.

Then along came Beck and Hattie for Gordon to deal with. And Celia. All because of Timmon.

But that was another story. The Timmon problem had to be addressed right now. The time had come for Revenance and Revelation. Karma needed to call. It was time.

Gordon Tappenhouse Symthe could play any role easily. He'd played many roles, just like Cary Grant.

Today, he would be a butler. He pranced down the hall in his impeccable suit, an intimidating butler, carrying the letter to Timmon on a small, ornate silver tray. His nose was high in the air, a haughty look on his face, his silver hair perfectly in place.

Timmon was in his office, the one he'd been assigned to by Gordon. He was lounging at the ornate wood desk, feet out and crossed, hands clasped together, a dull, glazed, sleepy look on his face.

Gordon opened Timmon's office door and stepped in. He looked at Timmon.

No change. But Gordon the butler, would show no pity, even though Timmon had fled to Gordon's palatial, but mysterious private estate after his mother tried to burn down the Desert Store and murder Timmon. He'd been nesting here ever since. That was over a year ago.

Gordon sighed. He'd finally been forced to assign Timmon an apartment and office just to keep him from underfoot.

Since Gordon was a Master of Mime, he was particularly fond of explaining to people where he stood with them without using crude verbiage. Crude because spoken language could never convey the meanings that actions and body language could. Body language and certain noises were much more eloquent. Things like a sigh or a tiny, discreet cough behind a hand could be honed to express a multitude of meaning where mere words fell short. A low, questioning hum could set the world on its ear if done properly. Those modes of expression were much more effective and much more refined when dealing with others.

Gordon tapped his foot loudly and sighed loudly. But Timmon stared morosely at the blank sheet of paper lying on the desk in front of him and didn't look up.

Gordon coughed discreetly behind his hand. He hummed and waited. Timmon still stared at the blank paper. Gordon tapped a foot on the beautiful parquet floor again. Nothing. Finally, he sneezed very, very loudly behind his hand.

Startled, Timmon jumped and looked up at him.

"What?"

"Open this damn envelope, Timmon." Gordon raked his eyes over the unopened mail piled carelessly on Timmon's desk.

"Before you open your other mail. I'll wait."

Timmon stared at Gordon. He realized that Gordon had put up with enough. He knew Gordon could and would stand there waiting until hell froze over if necessary.

"I'm sorry, Gordon, for trying your patience," Timmon spoke contritely as he grabbed the envelope from the silver tray, hastily opened it and drew out a legal looking paper. It was a deed. A short note was attached to it.

"Come on now," it read.

Timmon fingered the paper. He knew it was an invitation to get the hell off of his ass and go do something besides mope around Gordon's house. He wondered who had sent it. Celia? William? Who?

He admitted to himself that this call to adventure had shown up just when he sorely needed a good, long road trip to clear his head. To somewhere he'd never been. Or ever thought of going to. Well, it was way past time to get off his butt. At least a year past time. He stared at Gordon, speculation in his eyes.

Gordon sighed. He knew what Timmon was thinking. Timmon was different in ways that Gordon paid close attention to. His Sight was almost holy. In some ways, Timmon was kind of a priest. Gordon and Timmon almost became peers. But Timmon's youth stood against him in the wisdom area. And, Timmon was committed to Celia, who Gordon was training.

Celia was an impulsive, reckless Amazon. A tower of power with an excess of hormones that needed to have her own way. Celia was adept at hiding out until she chose to show up. Celia was always impatient with the many gifts she carried, which she was well aware of.

She trained diligently with Gordon but with a view to going out on her own to conquer whoever or whatever got in her way. Including Timmon. Celia wanted no mentors, and she was only a student in order to learn how to better use her powers.

Celia was in love with Timmon. She was determined to bag him. Gordon grimaced at the word, but it was true. Celia had fallen in love with Timmon when she was a mere child. She'd stalked him ever since. As far as he could tell, Timmon was fond of Celia, but in no hurry to deepen the relationship.

But then, Timmon was never in much of a hurry about anything. He had no sharp edges, no need for instant gratification...except for food...and smell. Gordon smiled. Timmon's sense of smell and taste was legendary in their world. In the world of taste and smell, he was a golden child.

Timmon was thinking that a trip to anywhere would be a damn good excuse to get away from Hattie, Beck, and Gordon. They were dedicated to training in a way that he never would be. He recognized that fact shortly after Hattie and Beck were installed in Gordon's house.

Celia was Sighted too and nuts over training. Couldn't get enough of it. That's the only thing they parted company on. That, and she was very forward. *Very, very forward,* he thought. *Always pushing me. For things I cannot give. And may never be able to give.* He set those thoughts aside.

"William?" Timmon asked, looking hopefully at Gordon.

"Unfortunately, he can't go with you. This is your trip," Gordon answered, deliberately misreading Timmon's real question.

Timmon raised his eyebrows. Maybe the nightmares of the Desert Store burning would stop if he got on the road.

"Okay." he dropped his head and nodded at Gordon.

"Best get some rest, then." Gordon said.

That night Gordon made a sleeping potion and gave it to Timmon in warm milk. Gordon placed protection around Timmon to keep Timmon's evil mother Mina and her minions from finding him.

Timmon packed up and headed for Colorado. Refreshed and able to think straight again, he took his time driving to Colorado from California. He detoured and went sightseeing whenever the urge hit him. But detours didn't stop the insistent memories of his mother's hatred for him. The psychic confrontation with his mother at the Desert Store had happened over a year ago. But the amount of hate his mother had leveled at him and his beloveds during the battle still astounded and hurt him. The encounter wasn't impersonal like his other encounters with evil. It was his own mother and four sisters trying to kill him.

They lost. His mother, Mina, her lover Vance, Timmon's four sisters, and their minions had rushed back to their camp, packed up, and disappeared like a puff of smoke after they failed to destroy the desert store.

They had hoped to destroy Timmon, kill him, and his beloveds. But all they succeeded in doing was burning down the motel, restaurant, and every building but the Store itself.

Timmon didn't know where his mother, Vance, and their minions disappeared to. He didn't want to know. He knew they expected him to seek revenge, but he couldn't. He was too stunned, to hurt in the deepest parts of himself. He never wanted to see her or his sisters again. Still the question always arose. Why did she fear him and want to kill him so badly?

He had always been pragmatic about the situation with his mother and sisters before the desert store attack. He assumed that the problem was a war about their Sight. His mother used hers for Evil. He used his for Good. But the fight had escalated beyond human endurance and into a psychic war that didn't make sense.

He'd always assumed that he could cut off his feelings and move on because they were Evil. He had been living at the Desert Store with Mama and Cowboy Johnson parenting him since he was ten years old.

Avoiding his hurt, he'd fled to Gordon's after the battle was over and threw himself into work and learning. He convinced himself that his new reticence with Celia and others was caused by the dizzying speed of the big changes that had taken place in the Desert Store and most of his beloveds the past year.

When the battle was over and Mina, Vance and her minions had fled, Susan Sugar Diamond had turned to him.

"Oh! I know! We'll just rebuild!"

Timmon pictured the motel and restaurant and shook his head. "No. No more like it was."

"How about a school and a...church?"

She waved her hands around. She was still fired up from the psychic battle. She glanced admiringly over at sweaty, lanky-haired, bare-chested Matthew, who was standing spread-legged with a jubilant look on his face. Doing nothing. Just standing there as though that was enough. Standing there as if waiting to be admired and praised. Was he posing for her? Again? With a name like Susan Sugar Diamond, no wonder.

Timmon shook his head. Susan tore her admiring gaze away from Matthew and focused on Timmon again.

"A school? "Who for?" Timmon asked.

Inspiration struck Susan. "For orphans! We'll build an orphanage! You know, I was an orphan, too. So was Lana."

Timmon stared at Susan Sugar Diamond, world famous author, and her forever sidekick, Lana English. He examined their eager, flushed faces, stilettos, and tight, skimpy hooker gear. Their bosoms were almost bare. Their makeup had run all over their triumphant faces. Their hair was sweaty but still standing up. They were oblivious as to how they looked. They'd never been in a psychic battle before, let alone one they'd helped win.

He glanced over at Matthew and Perry. They were bare-chested and sweaty, smoke smudges and wet hair hanging in their eyes, holding stances like heroes in a bad B action movie. They had saved their women. Lana and Susan were ogling Matthew and Perry. Matthew and Perry were ogling Susan and Lana back.

Timmon looked around. The motel and restaurant lay in smoking ruins. Everything was gone except the little desert store, renovated from a little white-steepled church that once stood on the property.

Timmon thought of Avery. He couldn't let him down. This was Avery's legacy. The Desert Store sat dead center on a chakra. One powerful enough to best the Evil that had tried to destroy it today.

Yes. He would do it for Avery. Timmon studied the four eager faces in front of him. He pictured Cowboy Johnson and Mama and suddenly started laughing. They would have appreciated the irony. Life springing from the ashes.

Less than a month later, he signed the Desert Store and its entire property over to Susan Sugar Diamond, former orphan. Who else would know how to better build an orphanage?

He knew that Cowboy Johnson and Mama would like their place of power, their little store out in the New Mexico desert, actively doing Good once again.

That was the last time he remembered laughing over just about anything. He'd gone back to the ranch, showered, and cleaned up. Then he fled to Gordon's house and fell straight into a funk. Something in him was gone. And he couldn't get it back. That's why he was headed to a small town named Gitwell, Colorado, to examine a mysterious property deeded to him by mail.

He knew Gordon and William's busy, nosy hands were in this plot to get him interested in something besides his own misery. He didn't really care. Maybe they'd given him what he needed most. An interruption in his dismal, miserable existence. Maybe whatever they planned would help bring him back to at least a semblance of his former self. He sure as hell hoped so!

Timmon drove into the little town of Gitwell, Colorado, population 98, in Gordon's favorite, once immaculate, now very dusty Jeep. He headed for the over-dressed, dingy motel and checked in. It was the only one in town. His room was not very clean, and filled with cheap western décor. Horseshoes nailed to the wall by the door, spurs laying on a cheap brown table, and faded pictures of horses minus frames taped on the walls. The carpet was brown, dirty, and worn. A tiny bathroom with a shower he was barely able to turn around in. The bed looked lumpy and turned out to be just that.

He went to the Pardner's Bar for dinner. His was an extremely picky palate, and he detested inferior food. The stench of cheap beer and stale sweat permeating the bar didn't stop him from enjoying his meal. The cheeseburger and fries he ordered were lush and flavorful, as he'd suspected they might be. Most bars could be counted on to have good burgers. And, he didn't have to talk to anyone over the noise blasting from the jukebox in the corner. He took his time and drank a refreshing, cold beer before he paid his tab and left.

When he stepped out the door of the bar, something swooped down and swept by him. Something dark, whispering words that sounded like "Golly Man and son" as it flew by his head. He watched the black thing winging its way north. He shook his head. No need to get spooked. It was a bat, no doubt, he told himself. There was a lot of forest around here. That's where bats liked to live. Also, it was summer, their favorite time to bother people. Still, he stepped up his pace back to the dingy motel.

The next morning, he packed quickly and efficiently, and left the motel in relief. He made it a habit to never leave anything behind in a motel room for snoopy people to sift through. No one else need know he carried a small, efficient gun and a couple of small, handy knives. He headed out to his new mystery property to look it over.

Gonna' go travelin'
found sumthin' in my shoe
doan' need no map
'cause dat' sumthin' be
stuck in the corner of my blues

Chapter Five

The country road was dusty, narrow, with no potholes. No washboard avenue. Not bad, Timmon told himself. He drove until he reached a dusty lane, stopped, took out his map, studied it. He folded the map, tucked it back in the glove box, and took the lane.

A short time later, the air thickened with an ominous foreboding. He clicked off the radio. Voices surrounded him and the Jeep, whispering threats.

Timmon instantly threw up invisible shields so whoever it or whatever it was couldn't see him anymore. The whispers stopped.

He slowed to a crawl and studied the bare, flat land on both sides of the little lane he was on. Short grass. No trees or bushes.

He felt and heard the ominous humming before the house came into view. The humming noise grew louder, vibrating through the air, turning it cold, dank, and heavy.

Suddenly, something enormous rose in the barren field on the left. The noise was coming from it. He gasped at the shockingly high, huge, old gothic house squatting on a piece of flat land. No fences, no gates, no trees, no shrubs, no walkways. Nothing stood between the road and the monstrosity of a house squatting on the edge of a long, too flat field. Nothing to explain any of it. No signs, nothing. Just a huge ugly ruin of what was probably once a mansion. The stench of evil poured out of the structure. He could smell it clear out to the lane he was traveling. His heart began pounding.

Suddenly, the scent changed. The humming grew gentle. The scent of fine cinnamon and sweet sugar swept through the air. Timmon's sense of smell was one of his strongest Gifts. He couldn't help himself. He slowed to a crawl, pulled into the driveway, drawn in by the gorgeous, sweet scent. He drove slow, fighting the pull, but something Dark and magnetic and very old kept drawing him towards the old, ugly mansion. He belonged here. He just knew it.

The air thickened again. Timmon felt like he was driving through thick molasses, which indicated to him that there was some sort of time warp wrapped around the monstrosity in front of him.

He stopped by the front porch and climbed out and stood there, swaying, taking the enticing, sugary cinnamon smell in. He headed for the front porch steps. Home. Each hesitant step carried him a little closer to the decay in front of him. Suddenly, the porch changed. Little curlicues of what looked like white icing became layered heavily everywhere.

He stopped before he reached the first step and stared at the thin, round, metal handrail that suddenly appeared. It was the kind an old person might use to get up and down the steps. He suddenly knew that someone named Dolly had once used it.

Something behind the closed front door hissed. Timmon hesitated. A patch of dirty snow appeared on the ground even though it was summer.

His eyes followed the ripples of snow as they layered up against the house under one window. Okay. Enough. He got the picture.

Timmon backed away from the porch. Was the ruin a former hotel? The thing was definitely odd. It was shaped in peaks and wings and long windows. The vast, huge building and its overly decorated front porch acted like it was hiding something behind it, waited expectantly for him to come in, calling to him. He belonged to this place, somehow. He shuddered and forced himself to turn away.

He felt a touch on his shoulder. He jerked away and jumped in the Jeep, started it. He didn't bother backing up. He slammed the Jeep into drive, wheeled in a tight circle, and fled.

Just a heartbeat down the road, he felt strong waves of Goodness emanating from a little cabin on the same side of the road as the big, ugly mansion he'd just fled.

He guessed that it was once a tenant house for workers at the big house. Cheerful flowers bloomed around the shacky little place. The yard of the cabin was thick with strange looking objects. Some moved. Some whizzed. Some roamed. Some stood still, quietly waiting while other objects made a din of noise. There wasn't a square foot of open space, just paths through the odd objects.

The front and side yard of the cabin were overhung with huge ancient trees. Their long green branches swept the roof and grounds. Tall, sweet smelling grass grew randomly here and there, poking its way up through the hard ground.

The place looked like an artist's studio or like an old-time granny house with its clothesline, garden, and the rusted out old jalopy sitting to the side of the house as if trying to hide.

An air of wild sweetness was mixed in with the Goodness emanating from the little place.

Timmon slowed down and hesitated. He wanted to pull in the driveway, just like he had done at the old ugly mansion. He'd better stay away. Move on. Curiosity drove him past the quaint cottage. He wanted to examine the mysterious property he'd been deeded. The property was easy to find. Fresh red survey flags were all around its border. Timmon drove onto his new property, stopped, got out and looked around.

Gentle quiet everywhere. He relaxed. Nothing to surprise him here. Tall pines to the back of the vacant land swayed in a gentle breeze. The ground felt solid and welcoming. The land seemed sweet and untroubled, lonesome, ready for company. It had been waiting a long time for something or someone.

He began walking, peace flooding his soul while his eyes examined the wildflowers, the trees, and the arroyo running through his new place. He felt at home. Peaceful. Powerful. He hadn't felt like this in a long time. *In over a year,* he thought ruefully. *There were reasons for all things,* he thought. *This land and I need to be together. We are going to do some sort of project, and we are going to explore further down that road.*

Timmon was used to taking his time and planning everything out. His Sight kept things orderly, his emotions kept him aware. His keen sense of smell alerted him to changes and nuances in any atmosphere he encountered.

Suddenly he pictured an odd looking cathedral on this land. Tall, crooked, and imposing. He grinned at himself. Who would visit it? Maybe just a little church? One like the desert store once was? Nope. The image came again. This property had been waiting for someone to do a certain thing on it for a long time, his Sight informed him. This property was centered in another Good energy chakra like the Desert Store was.

When he was done, he climbed into the Jeep and drove back down the lane. He found himself pulling into the driveway of the cabin he'd passed. He parked the Jeep beside the old beater station wagon parked under the tree.

A small, white-haired old woman stepped out on the porch. Timmon sat in the Jeep and studied her. She studied him back. She looked older than this ancient, rocky land and somehow younger than a daffodil.

Timmon sniffed the air. A scent of homemade cookies. Lemon or vanilla. Lean, sweet herbs, something stewed down to a sugary, fascinating something. The compelling odor made him salivate. He realized he was hungry. Very hungry. And he wanted to eat something the old woman had cooked. Or baked. Or roasted. Whatever. Anything.

She watched him climb out of the Jeep. She said, "Welcome. I'm Lou. Come on in the house, away from out here."

He understood. It felt like there were unseen ears listening outside the perimeter of odd things placed everywhere around the cottage. He made his way carefully toward the porch, not touching any of the odd things he walked through.

Shem stepped out on the porch, letting the screen door shut silently behind him. He stood behind Lou at her shoulder as they watched the golden-haired, lean man make his way carefully toward them like he was walking through a minefield. Lou laughed.

"He's right, you know. Everything out there could harm him."

She laughed again.

"But only if he was bad. Just a little bit of harm."

She shrugged. "Won't do to let 'em think they got easy pickins."

Timmon reached the porch and stopped.

"Come on in."

Lou pointed at Shem.

"This here is Shem. He's new to the place, too."

She turned and led the way into the cottage. Timmon sniffed the air in the cabin. His Sight and keen sense of smell told him a beautiful fairy tale. Cookies. Buttermilk and lemon cookies. Cookies so soaked with briny lemon that they split open in the oven just to get away from themselves. Baked in a stove that took firewood. Hidden in a canister behind some dishes. Taken out only on special occasions. He hoped this was one of them. If not, he had cash. Plenty of it. He hesitated. She looked to be a tough old bird. Might not try buying.

What do I have to do to qualify? he thought, his mouth watering. He stepped inside and looked around. One big room with a smaller one to the back. Typical of the old-time tenant houses. He'd seen a few when he was growing up. Lived in them, actually.

Memories of his family and his mother rushed in. He shoved them away. This was a new age, a new time, and this cozy little cottage smelled of magic and lemon cookies. Behind those scents, the cottage smelled of stringy, tough Goodness. He stared at Lou. Or was that her?

Lou watched him, assessing his mixed reactions.

"Some of it's me. Some of it is Shem. That's true. Want coffee?"

Timmon nodded warily. So, she could read his thoughts? Coffee wasn't one of his things. Never was. Chocolate was. And certain specialty teas. But everyone drank the vile stuff, it seemed. And any time of day, too. He nodded again, bitterly accepting his fate.

Lou stared at him, then laughed. She turned to the refrigerator and took out a bottle of milk. She poured milk into a tall glass quickly, causing the milk to foam up. She placed the milk jug back in the refrigerator and reached behind some things. Suddenly, the smell of hard core lemon crackled through the air.

Shem jumped up from the table and backed up. Lou set the glass of milk down in front of Timmon, then carefully set a small plate with two cookies on it beside the glass of milk. Then she sat down in her chair across from him, rested her elbows on the table, and waited.

"Shem, git' you and me a cup of coffee," she ordered, without taking her eyes off Timmon.

Timmon ignored both of them. He was too busy swirling his first cautious sip of rich, fresh milk around in his mouth. The nuances of contentment and fresh nature, clean and untroubled, drifted across his palate. He swallowed and sighed blissfully.

The acrid, enticing cookie scent almost shocked him after the placid taste of the fresh milk. He stared at the cookies, ruminating. Two small innocent looking cookies, split and busted open while baking, emitting the sweetest, most acidy scent of concentrated lemon he'd ever smelled.

He was afraid of them. They were small landmines designed to kill him if he touched them or ate them. His stomach quivered in fear as his hand involuntarily hovered over the plate.

Shem placed a cup of coffee in front of Lou. He pulled a chair over by the kitchen window and sat on the edge of it, watching Lou and Timmon, his green eyes wary. He could get away quick, if needed. He knew where the back door was.

Timmon picked up a cookie and slowly, very carefully lifted it to his mouth. He took a tiny nibble, much like a scared rabbit. Surprise and delight warred for places on his face. He popped the rest of the cookie into his mouth, chewed, and swallowed. Gasping, he grabbed the glass of milk and downed it.

Then he grabbed the other cookie, popped it in his mouth, jumped up, and headed for the refrigerator as he chewed. He jerked the door open, grabbed the pitcher of cold milk, and drank from it. Lou cackled as he staggered back to the table with the pitcher and sat down.

"Got any more of those cookies?" he finally asked hoarsely.

"Looks like you've had enough for now," Lou said.

"May I have the recipe?" Timmon asked.

"Nope. They's more than what you might think in them."

"What's in them?"

Timmon sloshed milk into his glass, then gulped it down.

"Not tellin' jist' yet," Lou answered. "Anyways, nothin' that will harm the likes of you."

Timmon sighed with relief, then he became alert.

"Why "the likes of me?"

"Jist' 'cause," Lou retorted. "None of your business."

Timmon let it go. His tongue was still burning. He grabbed the pitcher and drank from it again. He murmured. "This milk is absolutely delicious. Is it fresh from a cow? Do you have a cow?"

Lou nodded. "Bessie. Out in the barn."

By this time, Shem had moved back to the table. He and Timmon looked each other over.

Lou cackled again. "Either one of you boys know how to milk a cow? I need somebody to take over part of my chores."

Shem and Timmon both stared at Lou. They shook their heads, wary looks on both their faces.

"There's a lot to learn around here, boys. You'll see."

"That your vacant land down the road?" Lou asked Timmon.

"Yes."

"Better get a move on and git' that church built right quick. Ain't much time left." Lou said to Timmon.

Lou stood and walked out on the front porch. Timmon and Shem followed her. She led the way around the house again. Both Shem and Timmon followed carefully. She stopped at the edge of the field and pointed to Manfred's Folly.

"There's what we got in store for us, boys. There's where the fight is gonna' be."

Later that night, Lou peeked in on the two boys sleeping in their beds. She'd fed them real good on cornbread, green beans, and large, butter basted steaks cooked well done. They'd chewed hard and wore themselves out eatin'. She didn't give them any sweets, for that would have kept 'em up another hour. They'd winked out like lights as soon as dark fell. They were plumb wore out, jist' like she wanted.

That's okay for right now, but they'll hafta' plan on losin' some sleep later, she thought as she dimmed the kerosene lamp on the end table in her sleeping quarters behind the curtain.

When it lowered to a dull glow, she nestled into the featherbed on the old, lumpy couch and pulled an afghan over her shoulders, closed her eyes, and dreamed of the man that looked like Cary Grant. She started arguing with both herself and him again, listing her faults.

Her temper had shortened over the years. She was an old grump now who watched her wordy mouth real close, but sometimes it just flew open and gave somebody, anybody, sixteen kinds of hell.

Then she whined. Besides, she was allergic to the flowers she grew. She couldn't eat hardly anything but biscuits. No spicy foods or too much butter from Bessie. No booze. Allergic to that, too. She fell apart emotionally at the drop of a hat, 'cause of her no good Papa. Without a proper Papa to start off life with, and her putting up with mean, stupid brothers, why should she trust any male authority figure, especially that Cary Grant man?

Another part of her spoke soothingly. *Look at Braxton,* it said smoothly. *He was a good man and helped you in every way. I'm lonely, I need another nice man in my life.*

We're too old! Lou argued.

No, we are not! What about that nice Cary Grant man you visit in your dreams just so you can bitch to him about your so called pitiful life? He seems kind. And he's very handsome, too. I could fall in love with him!

The lonely part of her that hoped for a companion shut up and turned away. Lou didn't know where that part lived. She didn't have its address. But it had hers. And it had its final say.

Louise Hope Cornfield began snoring. Her guardian angel watched Lou fret in her sleep. With compassion, the angel reorganized Lou's memories, causing Lou to refresh herself in her sleep with memories of being a freckle-faced, pretty, brown-haired girl who ran under the summer sun without a care. A young girl who washed her hair in tender rainwater pouring through the down spout at the corner of the house when it rained. A girl who ate beans and biscuits and fried potatoes and thrived on them.

A girl who became a friend to Nature, to the trees and the flowers instead of to people. That girl sat on a porch step with her angel beside her and watched the fireflies with delight until she, too, fell asleep.

I seen a bat flyin'
round and round dis' room.
gotta' git' outta' here
'cause it's gonna' land
real soon.

Chapter Six

Hattie and Beck

Gordon was exasperated. Hattie and Beck caused no end of trouble for him. Training those three brats, Celia, Hattie, and Beck, with Timmon not available to buffer their nonsense, was taking it out of him. Thank God he didn't have other students to bother with right now. Those three were more trouble than a whole room full of curious ghosts! Enough!

Hattie and Beck were constantly on the move. They didn't light anywhere for more than a few minutes. Beck was a Forest Whisperer. He'd incited the trees around Gordon's house to riot. The trees and the woods around his property were closing in on the house. They were moving around on the beautiful, formerly spacious grounds of his gorgeous, mysterious estate. He'd scolded Beck, the Forest Whisperer, but to no avail. Beck just shrugged and grinned at him. "You should negotiate a deal with them." he said.

Then there was his huge house. It had taken up some very bad habits, thanks to Hattie. It griped daily about its own personal problems. It creaked and groaned and locked doors, moved rugs and switched off lights whenever it took a notion to.

Hattie was a House Whisperer. She informed Gordon that the huge, expensive house he had built so carefully, wanted its own independence, and worse, had needed it for a long time. Hattie informed him that he should negotiate with his house as to its needs and compromise with it.

Gordon ordered Hattie to make the house stop acting up, or he would call in a wrecking crew and start all over. Hattie was aghast and huffed off. The door slammed shut behind her on its own. That night, the floor in his bedroom somehow rolled and tossed him out of his bed onto the hard floor while he was innocently sleeping.

To make matters worse, his dreams had gone bad. A mysterious woman named Louise visited him at least once a night for a few short minutes and bitched him out. Her complaints were endless. Louise deliberately made herself out to be much older than she was. She was Sighted and Gifted and short-sighted and ornery. She glared at him every night with weary eyes.

"I need a rudder," she always complained. "Where the hell are you?" Then she disappeared.

"Between Beck and Hattie raising hell every day, Timmon's misery, and now Louise bitching at me at night, I'm ready to get the hell out of here and leave them to it!"

"What the hell am I supposed to do about her?" he asked himself each night after Louise left. Yet Gordon found himself strangely awed and interested by the dream woman's magnetism. He wondered what the hell she meant by rudder. He looked it up. It meant something that needed steering. Guiding. Well, he could agree with that. Something vertical. Women carried the vertical energies. Maybe she just needed a mentor, a rudder.

But he instinctively knew that without passion of some sort, without some kind of love attaching Louise to the rudder, she was doomed to living a smaller life than she should have.

Strangely enough, he felt pity for her dilemma. He knew what it was to have to accomplish everything all alone, too. But he was successful, where evidently, she was not. Maybe deserved a hand, a good friend, a mentor, a rudder. He hoped she found one.

Maybe his dreams meant that he would meet her someday and become her mentor. Lend her a helping hand. He pushed thoughts of more away. He was old, but he still stayed mightily attracted to Louise. Maybe he'd met her before. What wasn't he remembering? No wonder he needed a long vacation!

Then Timmon had called, and Gordon got lucky. He'd sent Hattie and Beck to Colorado to help Timmon out. His house and the trees and forest stopped their rebellion and stayed still and quiet. Back to normal.

House behaving. Woods and trees behaving. Beck. Hattie. Timmon. All of them gone! Celia was back with her mother in Carolina. Gordon envisioned placid days of relaxing leisure after they left. He could return to cataloging his books on alchemy or do this or that while leisurely sipping his favorite imported teas.

He sighed and relaxed. Went to the kitchen. Made tea. He wandered back to his study, tea in hand. He sank into his favorite big chair and sipped tea.

Then the phone rang.

Gordon picked up the receiver.

"Hello?"

Gordon was surprised. He was rarely surprised by anything. He listened to voice on the other end. When they finished speaking, he said one word. "*No*". and hung up.

The phone rang again a day later. This time the call was from a higher-higher up. It was a call he didn't dare ignore. He listened to the words without protest. When they were done speaking he said one word. "Yes." And hung the phone up smartly.

Furiously, he paced the study. Then the house. All over. Sucking in its peace and quiet.

He couldn't stay and enjoy it. He'd been ordered to follow Beck and Hattie to Colorado. And, he'd been told to get his ass in gear by a higher up! Well, that wouldn't do. He was furious.

He wasn't Beck and Hattie's keeper! Just their trainer. He'd finally, at last — mercifully — gotten rid of them. He'd sent them to join Timmon in Colorado. They were to help Timmon build a sacred lighthouse or some such something on his property.

Gordon didn't give a damn what Timmon was building. A lighthouse would be just fine. Didn't bother him that a lighthouse might be considered weird on a 9000 feet above sea level plot of isolated land. So what? Timmon was weird. They were all weird.

Well, so was he, he admitted to himself. Well, no, he wasn't. It just looked that way to ordinary people, because they didn't have Sight or psychic abilities worth a damn. Most people were too scared to do or learn what it took to develop them outside of their religious beliefs. And they never wanted to take responsibility for how they used their Sight once they gained it.

Gordon suspected that a certain family, whose members traditionally carried prophetic visions, had somehow put him on this schedule. But he didn't plan to keep to their schedule unless they told him what was going on. They hadn't offered to tell him why, and he needed to know before he did anything as rash as running off to Colorado, where the troublesome trio was, no doubt, up to something again.

He dialed his higher- higher ups, and said one word, *"No,"* again and hung up. Then he went his way, dismissing them from his mind. Gordon rested, strolled, listened to classical music and wandered his property. He stayed stubborn, enjoying his now obedient house and still, spacious grounds.

He refused to answer their calls for days. Then he got curious and answered the phone. He was shocked at who it was. It was Lily Jean Bloome and she chewed his ass out.

"You better get over yourself and make your travel plans right now! William can't do it. He can't help them this time. You have to do it. William has to have more time to recuperate," she'd informed him testily and hung up.

Amazed, he called her back. How did she know them? Or was it William who knew them? He liked them both and admired and respected their innocent love and wisdom.

She answered the phone. "What's the problem?" she asked tersely.

"How do you know about this?" he asked her.

"None of your damn business," she'd informed him and hung up.

Gordon was shocked. There must be more to the situation than he'd thought. He dialed Lily Jean Bloome's number again.

She didn't answer. He called again and again. Still, she didn't answer. Wouldn't. He just knew it. Worse, she knew he was finally getting the picture.

Bristling, he jumped up and paced through his now sweet house until he came to a resolution. He admitted to himself that although he didn't know what the hell was going on, it was time for him to do what was needed. He would have to go rescue the brats! Evidently, there was a big deal going to go down! And they needed him there for it. Mollified, he grinned.

Then he frowned. This was his home base. He was very attached to it. The trees were now staying put and the house was itself again. Beck the Tree Whisperer and Hattie the House Whisperer were gone. There was no one around to listen to the house and forests pity parties, and it felt real good! He wanted to stay home now that peace reigned in his house once again. He knew everything in this house and how it worked. He knew the magic residing inside and outside on his beloved residence. He was the one who made it work, after all was said and done.

On the other hand, he'd been ensconced here for a long time. Maybe it was time for a road trip to Colorado. They obviously needed him there, he thought smugly, someone with unmatchable skills, the patience of a saint, handsome as Cary Grant, with matchless manners. He hoped to put his mime skills to good use, as the relief of any opportunity of being elegantly different was always welcome. Maybe he would go. But he needed a sign first.

Got a few surprises
waitin' in store
for dem' that crosses
dat' line drawed
'cross da' floor

Chapter Seven

Timmon

A few days after he moved in with Lou and Shem, Timmon called Gordon from a little grocery store located about twenty miles from Gitwell.

"Hello?"

"It's me. There's a lot going on here. I'm staying with a lady named Lou instead of in Gitwell. The deeded property is fine. Loaded with Goodness. Probably another small, positive Earth chakra. Lou is teaching me and another guy named Shem all kinds of stuff. Most of it has to do with methods used to ward off evil.

I don't know where this is all going, but I am interested in who owns that old mansion, that odd building out on Route Nine before you get to my property. It's not a nice place. I have to pass it to get to my land, and Lou's cottage is next door to it. That monstrosity sets down the road from Lou's place. Can you find out what you can, and I'll call you back later this afternoon?"

Gordon said smoothly, "That won't be necessary, Timmon. Hattie and Beck are on their way to Gitwell as we speak. They will take rooms at the motel in town. You'll want to get them out of that nasty little town as quickly as possible.

"You own the monstrosity property too. It's called Manfred's Folly. Your great great great grandfather on your mother's side bought the land and built that haunted place on it back in the early seventeen hundreds for his wife. He built what he supposed was a mansion on it. It's vastly haunted. Be careful. It has many strong components to it, like the hexagon room and the round tower. Don't go into the basement. Ever.

You received that notice about the nearby vacant land to get you there. Stay away from Manfred's Folly and wait for Hattie and Beck. I'll be along soon."

Then he said a strange thing before he hung up, a thing Timmon was to remember later.

"Get the history of Manfred's Folly from that person you're staying with. You said her name was Lou? Is that short for Louise? I need to know. Also, stay away from your relatives, Timmon, stay away from them."

"What?"

"You heard me. I send that part of this message to you with resonance. Get back to me on the Louise thing, ok?"

There were still a few more days left before he would have to leave for Colorado. He planned to enjoy his remaining solitude to the hilt. Books and music. Art. Good food. No company. No busy, babbling house, no wandering forest to deal with.

Gordon hung up. Timmon stared at the dead phone.

"Well, hell, how come I'm always the last one to know?"

He wandered out to the Jeep, a dazed look on his face. He was trying to put two and two together in his head and make it come out four, but it didn't work. Not yet. He climbed into the Jeep and headed back to Lou's.

William and Lily Jean Bloome

William was in his element. He lay naked, totally relaxed on the smooth white bed, staring up at the ceiling, watching the reflected ocean water changing patterns as a sun warmed breeze drifted lazily through sheer white curtains.

Lily Jean Bloome was in the shower. Happily, he reflected on the late love in life dilemma so many older people faced and turned away from in fear. Lily was the one to bring him back to life. He'd never have done it on his own. Now his life was beautiful. He dozed, then woke up. Something was nagging at the back of his mind.

It had been building for days and bothering the hell out of him. He sat up straight. He knew now what it was.

Just then, Lily Jean Bloome stepped out of the bathroom, a towel wrapped around her. She saw the look on William's face and sighed. The cat was out of the bag. He had figured it out.

"No, William, this is Timmon's problem to deal with. And he has Beck, Hattie, and Gordon heading to Colorado to help him. Celia will come along later. All of them are gifted with different kinds of Sight. They are well trained for this kind of confrontation."

William studied her as she calmly dressed herself. Then he swung himself out of her bed and pulled on a pair of faded jeans over his underwear. She watched him shrug into a T-shirt, slip his feet into sandals, slide the patio door open. The sound of the ocean poured into the room. He stepped out onto the deck, closed the door behind him and headed down the sandy beach.

Lily Jean Bloome knew there was nothing more to say. She'd blown her cover out of love for him. She knew he felt betrayed. Now, he would do what he needed to do about it. She went to the kitchen and brewed herself a cup of the special tea she kept for these occasions.

Matthew's empty beach house came in sight. William stopped at the house and sat down on a rock He was as confused as a human could be.

He felt betrayed to the very depths of his being. Algestine had betrayed him. Led him on. Now Lily Jean Bloome had lied to him about who she was. He'd trusted her completely. With his soul. With every particle of his being. Who the hell was she? He stared out at the ocean, not seeing it. He fought with himself for awhile before he came to the bottom line.

Maybe it was okay. Maybe it was just that there was more to her than he'd imagined. He'd have to accept that she might be even more to her than he had expected to love. He had to get over himself.

He stood up and strolled back down the beach without giving Matthew's house a second thought. He knew where the spare key was. But Matthew wasn't home, anyway. He was away at the Desert Store with his son Perry. They were, no doubt, hanging out with Susan Sugar Diamond and Lana English, screwing, yelling, and fighting while renovating something or another.

Besides, there were questions to be answered and food to hunt up. Suddenly he was hungry. And, he was considering prospecting again. Alone. That's one thing Lily Jean Bloome didn't know everything about. Maybe that was an answer. But he needed to replenish his inner vitality first. Bring it back up to par. He needed a beer. He trudged on down the beach, headed back to Lily Jean Bloome.

She had a cold beer waiting for him. He sat down in his chair, picked up the beer. It went down smooth, settling his insides. *Sometimes you just have to let the emotional go and take care of your physical well being. Address that first. The rest, later.* William thought.

He sniffed the air. It smelled like steak. His mouth began watering.

"Are you cooking steak?"

He looked at her.

"Yes."

"Thank you." he said.

He sat back and closed his eyes. Her eyes filled with silent tears. She willed them away.

"You're welcome." she answered softly.

The ocean breeze blew softly through the windows, bathing them in negative ions. The day was warm but cool enough in the house. Life would go on. But it would be different now.

Louise Hope Cornfield

Lou sat on the porch in her rocking chair, thinking hard. It was after midnight. The boys, Shem and Timmon, were sound asleep in the back room.

She used to like to walk. Like Shem did. She'd walked until she became a missionary and got the first old rust bucket gifted to her by the church. They'd insisted she learned how to drive. Her first rust bucket had been an Oldsmobile. A land yacht large enough for her to live out of. It had a back seat the size of a small bedroom, a trunk the size of a large closet. She slept like a baby on the richly padded leather back seat.

She loved driving fast cars. She liked good-looking cars, too. Big shiny chrome laden cars. The kind of cars they made back when she was a girl.

Well, here she was. An old bird living in a cabin nine thousand feet above sea level, living in a state with too damn many mountains, not enough grass, and way too many snotty, upper-class rules. And people who didn't want to know anything other than conquering the mountains and the land. But the cabin came with a price. It stood close to an evil mansion. Trouble again.

Her thoughts turned to men. One in particular. Bran. She'd had a good life with him. He'd been a good rudder, leading her through troubled waters, smoothing her path for her. Bran understood that she had to follow her Sight, do what it said. He had no short-sighted, bossy male ego raring to impose a path on her. Her chosen Path was her number one love, and he'd accepted that fact and admired her for it. Well, that was a long time ago. Was he going to be the only man to ever be in her life?

She was lonely. She needed a companion. Not a female one either. They gabbled on in high voices and tried to rule over you by helping too much. No. She needed a man. She began rocking.

Well, at least she wasn't alone for the time being. Two boys in there sleepin', both with different gifts of Sight. She knew instinctively that the boys would stay until hell froze over to help fight the comin' trouble.

The boys, Shem and Timmon, helped with all that she asked.

They all knew something bad was going to happen. Lou just hoped they would be allowed to live through it. She was teaching the boys all the stuff she knew as fast as she could.

Suddenly, she was exhausted. She went inside, lay down on the couch behind the curtain, and pulled her afghan over her shoulders. Her last thought was resentful and hot. *"At least you could have given me another nice man to help me out."*

Gordon

A few nights later, Lou was sitting in her rocker on the porch again. The boys were in bed, sound asleep. She'd kept them busy all day with canning and cookin'.

She chuckled and slipped the hidden timepiece out of her apron pocket. Delicate and antique looking, it was made of pink gold with ornate scrolling around its edges. It gleamed in the night light. She opened it. Both hands stood at midnight. Tiny bells sounded. The witching hour. The time for magic.

She sighed, closed the watch, and slipped it back into her apron pocket. She'd found the magic watch laying on a street in a little Wyoming town when she stopped to gas up and grab a sandwich from a diner. She'd been on her way to Colorado.

She closed her eyes, remembering that day. The round, delicate pocket watch lay glimmering in the sun on the empty sidewalk. She'd leaned over and looked closer. The dust of ages the watch was covered with parted and she saw etchings of runes and symbols.

She snatched the watch up and opened it. Suddenly, the world around her changed. She stood in the center of a large ring of pink, lovely scented flowers. She drew in a long breath of delight, spread her arms wide, and turned in a slow circle. Her allergies to flowers didn't kick in at all. It was delightful!

Suddenly, she heard a deep, masculine voice.

"Pardon me, Ma'am. Allow me to introduce myself. My name is Gordon," the voice said. "Be careful where you're dancin'."

Her eyes flew open and she was back on the dusty sidewalk in the little Wyoming town. She looked left and right. There was no one around. Hastily, she snapped the watch shut and slid it into her pocket.

She never forgot the man's voice that had spoke to her. It was an unforgettable voice. One laden with nuances of amusement and depth. Smooth and deep. Gentle and magnetic. She whispered the magic watch man's name. Gordon. That was a couple years ago.

Gordon

Gordon liked to drive his Jeep, but Timmon was using it. Annoyed at his lack of foresight in lending his favorite toy to Timmon, who might wreck it or never bring it back, Gordon ordered a new Jeep in fire engine red. Then he changed his mind. Better to go into an unknown situation discreetly. He changed his order to a 1967 CJ5 black Jeep. At least it was a classic. When it was delivered a few days later, he packed tidily and efficiently and set out for Gitwell, Colorado.

That night, he stayed at an expensive, cozy Inn and dreamed of the woman named Louise again. But this time, the dream was different. Louise told him she didn't need him anymore. Her words offended and hurt him.

He grew even more determined to figure out who the woman who had pestered him in his sleep for the past couple of years was. He chanted a sleep spell and fell into a heavy sleep.

Memories flooded him. He groaned in spell induced dream-sleep. At last, he remembered who she was to him. It had been so long ago. He'd forgotten. Maybe the Lou Timmon was staying with was her!

In his dream, drove down a road where a red and white striped revival tent had been erected in a barren field. He drove across the field and stopped by the tent. There was no time to waste. He jumped out of the Jeep and ducking under a tent flap, he hurried to the stage. The woman named Louise was sitting on a corner of it, hands folded, swinging her legs and humming. As he reached her, she looked up at him.

"Hurry!" she whispered. "Manfred's Folly! I need you!"

Early morning found Gordon speeding toward Gitwell as the crow flies as much as he could. Short cuts. Bad roads. Anything to get there faster. No time to waste. No more procrastinating for either one of them. Louise What's Her Name was there. She didn't know it yet, but there was a much bigger picture to be explored between them when whatever the problem was had been handled.

In his dream last night, he had spontaneously leaned over, grabbed her up, held her close and kissed her thoroughly before he ran from the tent. He grinned to himself at the surprised look of wonder and delight on her face before he ran.

He speeded up. Right now, she needed his help. They all did.

"Dere' be things that Darkness
cain't take from us.
cause' dere' be things don't
belong to Darkness,
jist' like dere' be things that does
belong jist' to de' Light."

Chapter Eight

Where the engine flew to be with you
counting rhymes a do do do do
On its way to trouble ahead
Just be glad if you don't end up dead
a do do do do do do
double said two

Crazy Jack was a curmudgeon, like Lou, but
the best news was that he never went near
Gitwell, where his ex-wife lived happily in open
sin with the lumber company owner's son.
Instead, he drove to Bellville, a town forty miles
in the opposite direction to get supplies.

Crazy Jack was an old-time prospector. He
still expected to strike it rich. He was hale and
hearty with a good mind, but his ex-wife had
convinced everybody in Gitwell that he was
crazy. Nuts. A psycho. That's where his
nickname came from. Unearned and
undeserved, Jack said. Lou agreed. But the

moniker stuck, he said. Jack couldn't shake it. Everywhere he went, people called him Crazy Jack. He was sort of used to it now, he said.

Lou and Crazy Jack had met at the Belleville Hardware Store. They both showed up at the same time to pick out nuts and bolts and other odd things.

"What ya' need all that weird stuff fer'?" Jack nosily inquired of Lou's large purchase of strange odds and ends.

"To make special things with," Lou answered cautiously, looking around to see if anyone was watching them. No one was. "Protection things. I live in the cabin by The Folly."

Jack looked surprised. Then he nodded sagely. "The Folly's a bad place, all right." He studied her. "What the hell are you doin' there? Why don't you move on? It would be …safer…some say."

Lou looked him up and down. Jack looked like a dried-out old tree, withered, except for his long beard, which ended just above a large belt buckle that looked like it weighed ninety pounds. She shook her head with determination.

"Nope. Ain't nobody gonna' drive me off my own property."

"You own Folly's Cottage?"

Lou nodded. "Do now. Got it deeded to me."

Jack refrained from asking any more questions, though she could see it cost him.

"Well, good luck," he finally said, pulling off his cap with the John Deere Label on it and scratching through silvery, long hair that didn't look too clean. When he finished, he put his cap back on and turned away. He took a couple of steps and turned around again.

"Look, if you need anything, I live out on the old Stimson place. You take Route Fourteen straight to the lane after the biggest oak tree you ever seen. Turn right, and you'll find me. Go slow, or you'll miss the turnoff."

"Thanks," Lou said. "I'll take you up on it when it is needed. And it will be."

He nodded.

"Reckon it will. Time will come," Crazy Jack agreed. She watched him walk away. Lou stared after Crazy Jack. She'd met a Sage that day. Now that same Sage was protecting her cabin for her.

Lou, Shem, and Timmon stowed their luggage and sleeping bags in the Jeep and got underway. They waved goodbye to Jack and left. They cruised carefully past The Folly. There were more vehicles parked out back.

Crazy Jack would be tending the cabin while they went foraging for psychic tools to fight with. The fight would take place at Manfred's Folly. They knew that much.

Lou hoped the cabin would still be standing when they got back. It should be, since Crazy

Jack was only coming out twice a day to feed the chickens, gather eggs, and milk Bessie.

The three of them rode in the opposite direction of Gitwell for a few hours. Then they turned north, headed to the little, mysterious magic shop they'd heard about. It was said to be located high in the mountains where snow lay pristine and undisturbed by the doings of people year-round. No snowmobiles allowed. Nothing with a motor.

Those rules kept the place in pristine silence. Silence that myths were made of. They would have to walk or ski or something part of the way. The gear they might need was in the back with their luggage. They hoped they were prepared enough.

Stories abounded of mysterious beings and unusual happenings in the area the store was in. Nothing ever proven. That same area was famous for whiteouts and odd events.

The magic shop located there was supposed to carry tools of Goodness to fight Sighted wars. The buyers' instincts, or whatever powers they possessed, led them to its location. The place stayed lost to all others.

Timmon wanted to stock up on gemstones. He'd used the last of his supply to neutralize Vance and Mina's camp not far from the Desert Store back in New Mexico.

Also, he would also needed old, cold metals wrought and embellished with gemstones. Metals and stones that formed alliances with each other, enhancing the powers each held. Magic that would take the heat out of the upcoming battle. Suddenly he realized that he was afraid of heat, of fire. Ever since his mother and her minions had tried to burn down the Desert Store and murder him. He swiped a suddenly unsure hand across his forehead.

He said, "I don't know about you two, Lou and Shem, but I personally don't know near as much as I should about the use of tools to fight psychic battles. I grew up around a bunch of healers at the store who healed people stopping for gas or a bite to eat. Mostly they didn't know they were being healed. A lot of healings in disguise took place. Hugs or Cowboy Johnson's music or shaking somebody and pretending the one that did it just had a friendly fit of some kind.

My desert store family had all kinds of Sight-gifts. But nobody much used physical tools to wage psychic battles. Except for Normaine. But somehow, I think her mobiles might not do the trick this time.

I have been leery of another battle ever since the last one I was involved in a bit over a year ago."

He glanced over at Lou and Shem. They didn't know his history.

"I'm not a coward, by any means. I've had to take part in psychic battles most of my life. But I've been recovering from the battle I was involved in last year, and still have problems from it. So I don't know how much of myself I can rely on to get me through another battle with evil successfully."

"What happened?" Lou asked.

A long silence went by as the three of them rode north, searching for the magic they would need to fight off the evil waiting for them to return.

"My mother's name is Mina. She is Sighted and has much power. She turned to the dark side when she fourteen. She hates Goodness and the Light. She has become more and more powerful. She joined herself to an evil man and his cult, and they tried to burn down the Desert Store, and murder me and a bunch of other people."

"Wow!" Lou said. They rode in silence a few minutes. Then Timmon said, "I'm having trouble getting past a broken heart, for she is my mother. Or maybe was. I don't know where she is now or whether she is alive or dead. And don't want to know."

Shem said, "I don't know where my mother is, either. She ran away from home when I was twelve. I don't blame her. She left so she could survive my low life, selfish, evil stepfather. I haven't seen her since. She disappeared. I have been looking for her for a long time.

"Damn!" said Lou. "And I thought my mother was bad for putting the Dark Hex on me when I was born!"

"What is a Dark Hex?" the boys asked.

"Oh. Well, I was a second twin. Mom didn't know she was having twins so she thought she was dying when I showed up. She put her fear in me and Dark Hexed me for life. Mr. Fear was my faithful companion and kept me stirred up until I learned how to disassociate myself into parts. I was fourteen back then. My Sight led me to a church and they put me to working as a healer for sweet baby Jesus. Then I became a missionary. That's why I like cars so much. Big land yachts. Fins riding high in the air. Chrome everywhere. Metal foot pedals that fit big feet. Leather seats. Oh yeah!"

Timmon and Shem chuckled. Lou continued. "Well, now we know stuff about each other. No pity parties allowed. Some things never get healed. Emotional intelligence will tell you that. It's emotional science. We have to live with some things. And they trap us. And we know it. It limits us and we suffer. Sometimes greatly. Once in a great while redemption something like it happens to us and we are set free of our trap. But not often."

They rode on in silence.

Then Lou said abruptly, "Stop the Jeep so's we kin' get out and walk around a bit, 'cause a car ain't no place to think things out on a larger scale."

Timmon pulled over. The three of them climbed out. They paced back and forth with no results. After awhile, they got back in the Jeep and drove on. They drove until sundown. They pulled over and set up camp beside a small creek.

They ate, then went to sleep early under the stars. The next morning, they set out again. They drove all day. Evening fell. Nobody had much of anything to say. But all three of them knew that greater forces were at work, directing their travels. Directing their thoughts. The next night, they camped out under another starry sky high up in the mountains. Lou slept in the Jeep, on the backseat, wrapped in heavy blankets.

The next morning, just at the crack of dawn, another Jeep came to a stop beside Timmon's. Gordon stepped out, posed languidly, and waited. Timmon sat up in his sleeping bag and peered at him.

"Gordon! What the hell! How did you find us?"

Gordon smiled and deflected Timmon's question.

"Masks. That's what we are going to need. Good, reliable masks to confuse and deflect the concentrated negative energies. That's what I'm thinking. Because we are dealing with a combination of both Good and Evil. The evil is more, which makes the outcome more unpredictable."

"What?"

Timmon shrugged out of his sleeping bag. Shem was up and folding his sleeping bag. When it was neat and tied, he went to the Jeep to put it away. Lou was hiding behind the Jeep.

"What's going on?" Shem whispered to Lou, sliding his gear into the Jeep like no one else was there.

"It's him! I know that voice!" Lou stuttered in a fierce whisper. Just then, Gordon rounded the corner of the Jeep. Lou rose, grabbed her blanket and wrapped it tightly around herself.

Shem looked at the two of them and wisely decided to disappear. This wasn't his meet up. One of his best gifts was knowing when he wasn't wanted or needed. Anyway, he had questions. He headed in Timmon's direction. Timmon was hunkered over the campfire, feeding it wood and making coffee.

Lou watched Gordon approach with her chin stuck out. He came to a smooth stop a couple feet away from her. Then he deliberately struck a pose that Cary Grant would have envied.

Lou sighed, her hungry eyes raking over him.

"Still got that watch?" Gordon asked Lou in amusement. She didn't answer.

"Still dancing when the magic takes you over?" he asked.

Lou quavered in a breathless voice, "Better leave me alone. I'm an ornery old woman. A curmudgeon. I'll have my way. I know exactly what I'm doing."

"Really?" Gordon drawled, drawing himself up to his full height, striking another elegant pose while grinning down at her.

Lou couldn't stop herself. She looked him up and down and over and over like he was a full gallon of the finest maple syrup in the world. Maple syrup was her favorite sweet. She didn't want a just a quarter of a gallon. Not a half gallon either. She wanted the whole damn gallon.

"Yep!" she said breathlessly.

"Well, how about I help you out. Make life easier, rosier?" Gordon drawled.

"I don't need your help." Lou snapped back.

"Yes, you do.", he persuaded in a gentle tone, as though he was talking to a child.

"It's so hard to be around someone who had such a good life, when I had sich' a bad one!"

Lou whined like a child at his tone, tears dropping from her eyes.

Gordon looked up, admiring the cloudless blue morning sky, giving her time to collect herself. She quickly wound down.

"Guess you'll have to get used to it." He said in a mild voice.

He grinned down at her, making a sound deep in his throat that sounded like the mournful cooing of doves. He studied her face and figure and drew his conclusion.

"Yes. You definitely need me. I hope you'll let the magic between us work this time. I hope you choose not to reject me because of your past and its negativity.

Don't do it to me this time. Let the negativity go. Be with me. We are Peers. I'm not better than you. I'm not your boss because I'm male.

You definitely do need me. Have for ages. You asked me to come here, and I'm here now, so let's not fight about it. Just give in, and let's both go do the job we came here to do. All of us. Together."

He swung his arm out to include Timmon and Shem, who were drinking coffee over by the campfire.

Lou stared up at him, swaying, remembering. A few nights after she moved into the cottage, she'd set down to rest in her rocker on the porch. After a while, she'd taken the timepiece out of her pocket and watched it bend and slide around in her hand. She'd looked at the time on its dials. Midnight. The witching hour.

She'd played with the watch until she learned to make time stand still for short periods of time. The round, gold pocket watch lay glinting innocently in her hand. She'd leaned over and studied it. The pocket watch was layered with etchings of runes and symbols.

"Time is wasting," a tender voice spoke from the watch, startling her out of her fantasy. It was the man called Gordon. His voice.

"Time you'll never get back. Hurry up and get on with it."

Startled, she had snapped the watch shut and slipped it back into her pocket. She stared out into the darkness and ruminated on what the familiar voice had said.

Gordon's voice had been firm, yet filled with warmth and affection. Things she had done without, it seemed like forever. She yearned to hear that voice again. Ever since she found the magic watch. She would never forget his voice.

And here he was. In person.

"No!" Lou gasped.

"How do you know your life wouldn't be better if it was turned upside down? If you went back in time and stopped coloring your hair white and began wearing clothes that fit you properly and started using creams for your skin again?

I happen to have several samples of a rose lotion with me that you might employ," Gordon said, producing a lovely little glass bottle full of pretty pale pink stuff from somewhere.

Lou stared at him, mouth open.

"Stop catching flies," he ordered gently.

Lou's mouth snapped shut.

"You've gone it alone for a long time," Gordon said smoothly. "No need to anymore. What if you gave up the Old Crone act and became just the Wise Woman you've always been? What if you claimed that you are an architect of Microcosmic Magic Wisdom? A Lovely Lady Magi with a magic timepiece?

You earned that watch, you know. You're already practicing the shielding arts with your mobiles and the objects around your quaint little cottage. What if you let your hair go brown again, leave it threaded with silver here and there? What if you let your freckles show and your pretty feet walk the warm earth with confidence? With me as your companion?

You've given up being a nomad, and settled into one place at last. But you chose yet another place where there is evil close by to be dealt with.

It is a habit that you choose to make a home where you have to go on yet another mission to rid the world of an evil. But I have news for you. Your new neighbors were there long before you took ownership of the cottage. That is a huge factor in this dilemma. Timmon's generations have always owned Manfred's Folly."

Lou's jaw dropped. She stared at him. He grinned down at her.

"Complicates things, doesn't it? You know, where there is great hate, there is usually great love, too."

"You sure are wordy!' Lou said resentfully.

"Yes. At times, I can be. Thoroughly," Gordon happily agreed.

"You know Lou, we're just renting space on this planet. We don't own it. But you are making it possible through your fine geometric architecturals to leave behind for posterity things that couldn't exist in this world without you.

Now, the time has come for you to do something that can't happen without you.

You'll be taking a strange path, an ancient medieval route to gather what is needed to defeat the evil thriving next door to you. The watch is the key you will use to inform changes. The journey will set you, Timmon, and many more people free from certain types of negative bondages. It is a great task that lies before you."

"I just don't see the point of forcing something on someone who doesn't want it," Lou said resentfully.

Gordon studied her. Then he said, "We're going to need masks. Good, reliable masks to confuse, confine, and disperse the concentrated negative energies."

"Evil, you mean, "Lou muttered.

"No. Do not forget for one minute that this is Timmon's family we're talking about destroying. His genetics are involved. This confront has been building since Timmon was ten. Now he is finally powerful enough. Rather than destroy, maybe we can set things right. Separate the evils, sort them out and send them on their ways, weakened. With a good spanking, one might say. Maybe we can accomplish our goals without destructive de-structuring," Gordon answered. "Darkness can't stalk and conquer all."

He glanced at his watch.

"We must be back to your ahh...cottage...that tiny temporary rustic abode...by five o'clock."

"What do you mean, temporary?" Lou glared at Gordon to keep from talking about the magic watch that twisted time into beautiful shapes she could dance in forever.

"You know exactly what I mean. You and I are meant to be together. But right now, this instant, we must hurry. I have something to give Timmon, and an errand for Shem to run."

He grinned down at her.

"You already have your gift from me. The watch. Remember? And now you must use it."

"I'm not one of your students!" Lou declared angrily.

"No, you're not. I've taught my students how to be still long enough to listen to the wind's voices. Wind voices are dictated by many things, you know," he drawled lazily, grinning down at Lou.

"Velocity, resonance, and so forth are taken into consideration. What mission is the wind on? Where did it pick up its cause? Anyway, I digress," he said as he crooked his elbow and offered his arm to her.

She glared up at him as she slowly placed a hand in the crook of his arm. Gordon looked down at his little lunar Shaman with amusement and affection. Yes, she remained a master of disguises. He'd never known her true age or look. Or her many names. Someday, he hoped to discover much more. Oh, yes.

Wastin' time befo'
aint' no time fo' dis' order now
git' yo're self back here
and go answer dat' door
it's the end comin' ta' git' ya'
ya' hears?

Chapter Nine

Mina

Time slid away from the woman Mina like a
snake slithering through green, violent glass.
There was no structure, nothing to grab on to.
Green glazed, pointed, sharp-edged icicles
hovered in exact rows on the porch edge above
her head. The green spikes could fall any minute
and pierce her brain, kill her. Pierce the top of
her head, shoulders, or back. Kill her.

She crouched lower and crawled along,
moving slowly through the crawl space that
turned left into the library where her mind lay in
ruins. She had to get to it. Fix it!

Every inch of her being was fear filled now.
She couldn't talk or think coherently any more.
Voices rang throughout the house, rising and
falling with nearness and then distance.

The voices were always on the move, fighting
with each other, restless, their inner fires
building toward an inevitable murder of

someone. They hunted her. They wanted to kill her. She shuddered.

She crawled back out of the library and began to climb the stairs on all fours. It took forever to reach her bedroom. She crawled across the floor, taking forever to reach the small window set high in the wall, and looked out. She needed to see that crappy cabin. She peered through the dust and dirt on the panes of glass. She dared not remove the dirt from the tiny window.

Blurred, but the cabin was still there. She sighed in satisfaction. What was in that place that called her to come to it. Well, she couldn't get there now. She was too tired. She turned away from the window, weaved over to the bed, climbed in, and fell asleep.

Her violent snores and snorts of rage were punctuated with curses. The curses permeated the sound barriers in the room, steeping deeper into their woven wreaths of violence.

Mina, once upon a time, was a free souled, innocent child playing in the woods. Now, she was an amoeba, a single-celled piece of rage with no memories of the other children she'd spawned. She lived on her hatred, focused it on Timmon. He was double Sighted because of her and that golden man. Timmon needed to die. They both did. How to kill them?

She fell deeper into the familiar dream. Darkness lurked in her soul, but she was still one of a kind when it came to her power and Sight. And she knew it. But Timmon, he was more powerful than her. He was filled with the white Light of Goodness. And the fool didn't even realize the extent of it!

She fell asleep and dreamed of the golden-haired man she'd taken into herself for one glorious time. He'd filled her with his Goodness. He had given her Timmon. It had happened long ago. When she was walking along the lane leading to the woods behind the old derelict house her and her man and kids lived in. Her man had stolen her when she fourteen. He raped and married her and she learned to use her Sight in his service. They were married with seven kids.

She'd swooned without a spark of protest into the golden man's arms, desperately seeking to live differently for just one split second. The golden man had held her up, then gently laid her down on a bed of grass.

The next thing she knew, for the first time in her life, sunlight and then moonlight entered her being. But the light didn't stay. It quickly left, taking the golden-haired man with it, leaving Timmon in her as a curse from the blending of the two kinds of Light, his and hers. She had risen, made herself presentable, and gone home.

But the pleasure from coupling with the golden man lingered in her, and she wouldn't let her man jump her like she was an animal anymore.

She refused to sleep in the same bed with him for months. She told him she had something bad inside herself and she didn't want him to catch it. He left her alone, using her words as an excuse to roam, to take his dark pleasures out on unknown, unwilling women.

Mina had the Sight. She knew what he was doing, but she turned away, relieved that it was someone else he was hurting instead of her.

When her man tried to molest her, her new scent drove him away. He slapped her and said, "You stink!" She washed, but the smell stayed, causing his sexual needs to vanish whenever she was near.

Her man took to staying on the road. Later, he began taking their boys with him, ignoring the newly born golden-haired boy and the stench the last child and his mother now carried.

Mina stirred angrily in her sleep at the memory of Timmon, for she was a daughter of Darkness now. She thrashed and moaned and fell deeper into a nightmare sleep. Timmon had to be destroyed. Then and only then would she become completely of the Darkness, the path she had chosen. Only then would the golden man let go of his hold on her.

Hidden high in the old mansion attic, a weathered flag with mysterious symbols embroidered on it, ragged and edged with mold, began flapping in the gathering wind, beckoning in the coming storm.

Crowell Goforth Restus
The Golden Father

The tall, spare man in the tan trench coat stepped down from the train onto the platform at the Denver Train Depot, suitcase in hand. Once upon a time, he'd been named Thebes Winters Restus. Now he was better known as Crowell Goforth Restus, Funeral Home Director (of a Another Kind in a Different World)

All Visitors Welcome!—the sign read.

Crowell G. Restus was visiting the area with a purpose. The purpose lay near the small town of Gitwell.

Crowell G Restus had witnessed many endings, many of which would seem entirely bizarre to those who didn't have Funeral Sight.

Those who did have Funeral Sight, anticipated and stayed prepared for peculiar endings.

They did the necessary rituals to prepare the dying for the handing over of the traveling spirits waiting with suitcases packed to leave for unseen realms.

They were used to the participation of other living things besides humans being a part of the package for most humans, and for the other beings residing on planet Earth.

Crowell G. Restus was a Master Funeral Director. People kept their distance from him without realizing what they were avoiding. He came from a place they hoped and wanted to avoid. But he wasn't interested in them. He had come from afar, and he was on a mission. He was here to collect what was due.

It was time. The Sighted woman he'd chosen to bear his only son, was still in existence. The woman was living on her last bit of life force. It would need to be replenished so she could move on into a new world. Only then would he be finished with her. He owed the woman that much.

Twenty years or more had passed. The Sighted woman had changed from what she was at their "chance meeting" years ago. Back then, she'd held the perfect amount of evil energy and unwilling, hesitant Good battling it out. A perfect balance for what was needed. She'd been teetering between Darkness and Light when he met her. He'd given his son into her body, into her keeping. But she kept trying to kill his son. In her stupidity, she might succeed.

He was here to stop her. Soon, her minor stint with evil would be over. She'd learn to not mess with power one way or the other. Here or over there. The gold in his hair glinted and sparked as he strode angrily away from the train depot.

Mina

Meanwhile, Timmon's mother Mina lay in her bed, high in her bedroom in the evil old mansion, dreaming of revenge. She dreamed of mocking Timmon, of enjoying the shocked look on his face when he found out that his real father was nothing but a stranger she'd laid with one time. Mina shouted at Timmon in her dreams.

"You're a bastard, Timmon! I took that golden-haired man into me one time, and we made you before he left. He fathered you out on that little lane that's a shortcut to old man Martin's place. He said he'd just got done workin' over there and was headin' out for a new place. And he needed to plant some more seed before he left. He told me he was Sighted, just like me. That's how come you got double Sight.

Suddenly, the golden man's voice, smooth and colder than ice, interrupted her most familiar, happy dream.

"Stop it."

The steely voice rang with clarity and authority. Mina's drug-induced dreams vanished. She wailed, "No! Come back!" to the lovely horror that fled. That horror was her most familiar companion. It was the only thing that insulated her from the Goodness of her childhood memories.

Mina fought it, but she quickly became distantly lucid and calm, dimly aware of the life she'd once led and who she'd once been. The pain of seeing her scanty, short-lived Goodness again took her breath away. She couldn't scream. No sound allowed. What sound was left from that time rushed into her being and settled there, carrying memories, both old and new, waiting. For the reckoning.

She shuddered. She knew the time of reckoning was upon her. Very soon, she'd be called on to reconcile the differences fighting inside herself. That fight would end her life. Good or evil. Which would win?

There was no mercy in the hated, familiar voice when it spoke to her again. She'd tried before, but was never able to place the voice. Now she remembered. She screamed.

"Shut up. Rove," the ice cold voice ordered her. "That means get your ass off of that bed and move!"

Mina tried desperately to retreat into the familiar, convenient cave of insanity she'd built, but it didn't work this time.

"You are not going to kill my son. There's no place left for you to run. No more lies for a bitch like you to tell. No place dark enough to hide you anymore. It's over. Now stand up and walk a bit, then go downstairs, slip out the library door at the far end of the hall, and go out back. Stay out there. Be damn quick and quiet about, too."

Mina obeyed. After a long time, she found herself in the field out back of The Folly. The wind was blowing, the weeds stinking with hearty, thriving richness. No voices. She tried to fall to the ground and lay there forever, but she stayed upright. She began tottering forward to meet her fate, swaying and hesitating between steps. Heading for the little cabin at the far end of the long field between The Folly and the cabin, shedding Darkness as she went, planning to find Timmon and kill him.

But the murderous, clinging pieces of her filthy Shadow shuddered and fell away, turning from her, clanging like iron bells, flowing like stinking oil. Mina tried to scream, to stop the pieces of Darkness, the collection of her many lovely evils, from leaving her. Mina's very soul adored and worshipped the dark, mean powers those pieces lent her. Not to care about anything or anyone else meant everything to her. Hate was all that was left.

Mina stopped and sniffed the air. Instinctively, she knew it wouldn't be long before she began to suffer in ways she'd never known before. The end was drawing near. She was not righteous. She'd just been what she was. That was all. It was almost over.

Suddenly, the golden-haired man appeared in front of her. Timmon's father. He glared at her.

She is correct. The righteous shall remain victorious, the golden-haired man thought grimly, kneeling in front of her. He opened a small, tan box. Quickly, he grabbed something out of it and threw it over her. A shroud. Golden scented wind whirled around her, cleansing and releasing the rest of the bad things she'd held on to.

Mina opened her mouth wide to scream, but no sound came out. The Shadow world, her beloved Darkness, no longer loomed over her, both protecting and battering her. The old, haunted mansion, her ancestral home that she and Vance had led their followers to, was no longer her respite. The Folly could no longer hide her. Mina was caught between the two great forces that rule life, forced in this time to recapitulate her services to each of them.

Incurious and uneducated about both Good and Evil, Mina's mind buckled under the strain. It went blank. There was nothing left. No Good or bad to ponder. No deeds to relive. No memories of her childhood or of her own children. Blessed silence. No voices either.

The golden man watched the woman wander, swaying and barely moving. She was headed to the cabin where Timmon was, to be exact. Just as the crow flies. But she wasn't a black crow, used to funeral pomp like he was, as she wandered her way towards her end.

It would take time. A long time for the woman he'd chosen and had hoped for much more than this miserable little ending, to reach her destination and end this horror.

Crowell Goforth Restus, son of Rex Winters Restus, an Honorable to the very end of the Three Winding Way Wars, stalked Mina until he was upon her. He tossed a turquoise necklace over her head. She didn't notice it, but her fingers crept up to smooth the cool beads. The beautiful round beads lay glistening across her chest.

He whickered under his breath in surprise as most of the beads turned to black ashes and fell away. She was more evil and powerful than he had thought!

He peered at the rest of the necklace. The beads dimmed, but stayed true blue. There was just enough left. It wasn't time for her to die. No, not yet. But soon, very soon.

An uneasy awareness ran through him like lightning. He'd been put on notice. There wasn't much time left for him here. It was hard enough to get permission for the time allowed for him to come here. Now it was almost time for him to leave.

He turned Mina back to the path she must walk. He watched her stumbling towards the little cabin. He wanted to do more, but it was time for him to leave. His time with the woman was up. Her fate rested in the hands of others. There was just one last thing he had to do in the short time he had left in this place. He waved his arms and disappeared.

Mina recapitulates the life she has lived

Though she fought it as best she could, Mina's mind began working again. Her insistence on being a primal, primitive, simple piece of hate began to fade as memories of her childhood flooded her mind.

She remembered the Goodness she'd barely touched, the Goodness that, once upon a time, influenced her childhood in long, sweet moments, bittersweet memories stored swiftly away and forgotten as soon as they were over.

No rainy days for Mina, days when she could sort through pleasant memories in leisure.

Born into a large, weak, cruel family, she was the only child to carry forth the Sight passed down through her mother's family. She'd been violently torn away from her family at age fourteen by an older man, a sex predator; he'd raped her repeatedly and forced her to marry him.

Her family didn't try to stop him. They let her go without any protest. Enraged at their weakness, that they didn't fight for her, defiantly, she left with him, and they traveled around the country, settling here and there.

Her man stayed constantly on top of her, worrying and shoving into her, and before long, there were seven children and no memories left of her Sighted Goodness.

Except for her memories of Timmon, her seventh child. Her last child. Timmon was golden-haired and looked exactly like the man who spawned him. Timmon had innocently kept his double Sighted Goodness right in her face with every breath he took. It was then that Mina began to hate her beautiful son. She didn't remember quite when the hate started, but it grew hot and fast.

Her man took the two older boys and went scavenging for no good things to do. He left the girls and Timmon to her. But by then, Mina no longer loved anything.

Angry and hate filled, Mina searched out negative power to aid her hate. She'd turned to her man's ways, aiding and abetting him with her Sight. She turned to the Darkness and welcomed it, for her soul stayed thin and hungry, angry and needy for any kind of power.

Mina lived alone inside herself now. Her man and sons were in prison for life. Leeza, her oldest daughter, had run off with one of Vance's devotees a while back. The other three girls slept around and whined all the time. Lazy, nasty things! They didn't stop at just hurting other people—they hurt her too!

Though she was Sighted, Mina was simple minded. She'd been astonished when her girls turned on her. Now they wanted her to die. At least her man and two sons couldn't get to her like Vance and her daughters. They couldn't use her Sight after they went to prison.

Over time, her strength had waned and she became more and useless to them. Her man and two boys in prison battered what Sight she had left with evil energies and thoughts. The four daughters she'd birthed and raised hated her and wanted her dead. She was constantly hammered by the evil vibrations they sent her way. And Vance despised her, wanted her dead, too.

Only Timmon, who didn't know how to hate, carried the Sight. And, he was double Sighted. Goodness reeked from him. And he loved her in spite of everything she'd done to him.

Mina wandered across the field as her hate rose in repugnance at the scant childhood memories of her Goodness. Her body didn't know what to do with the changes it was going through. She fell to the ground and puked violently.

She lay there, wanting her life to end. But the new forces that were taking her over stayed merciless. The battle for her sanity was ending. Now the battle for her soul was beginning.

Mina, mother of seven children, four daughters and three sons, the youngest being Timmon, dragged herself to her feet once again.

The only one who loved her was Timmon. Mina turned away from the cabin and staggered towards the dank darkness of the thick forest lurking behind The Folly.

She didn't want anything to ever touch her heart again. She didn't want to touch the dark misery living there, coiled like a deadly snake, toxic, ready to kill her.

Mina, mother, child, young maid and rape victim, didn't want to examine what had died in her long ago; what had never gotten buried, never was mourned. Instead she'd used her Sight to hate. There was such power in hate. And she'd lost her Goodness to it. No one had protected her. No one had tried to save her.

Even if she wanted to, she didn't have the power now to release her spiritual agony to its final resting place. She didn't have the strength to let it heal, either.

It was over. She stumbled closer to the forest and watched a tree lose its last leaf without knowing anything about winter or spring. Her seasons were gone. She stumbled along, heading towards the forest instead of the cabin where Timmon stood, hoping to avoid her destiny.

Shem the Walking Man

Something or someone was calling out to Shem. He strode away from the campfire where Gordon, Lou, and Timmon were hunkered down, discussing strategies about handling the evil living in Manfred's Folly.

Shem didn't know how far they would get with Lou staring at Gordon like he was the prize cake in an international bake off, with Gordon staring back at her, forgetting everything he'd just said. Shem heard Timmon say, "Focus, Gordon!" as he strode away. Shem grinned.

Shem knew all about walking. He'd been on the road most of his life. He figured life's little problems out quickly and best while pacing, walking, moving on. His philosophy was just keep moving. Shem was a walking philosopher. He knew all about moods and awareness and the beauty of Nature. He'd been awed into stupors at times by the gorgeousness of the Nature surrounding him as he traveled.

He never explained much to anybody about anything. Didn't need to. His speech was simple, full of deep meaning, so he didn't use it very often. His thoughts and words were private. It embarrassed him to explain things to anyone.

Nature had taught him and tended to him over the years, and he willingly lived under that domain, silent except to her whims. The more he learned, the more he knew he didn't know. That was easy to accept, for it left new places for him to discover. His life of seclusion was clean, sparse, and intensely fulfilling. He was content in a way that many others weren't.

His intuition grew stronger each time he time moved on to a new place. He needed people to help him keep walking, that was his only problem, for his was a life pilgrimage with no particular destination that he knew of. Well, he knew, but didn't want to think of his mother. Where the hell was she?

Right now, his intuition was on high alert. He was being called to go somewhere. He walked rapidly over a hill and out of sight of the others. Then he stopped, bent over, and deep breathed until he got a bearing on what it was.

His Sight opened up. Lou's house popped into his mind. He watched Crazy Jack peeling spuds in the kitchen. All felt peaceful there.

Then his Sight took him for a quick walk behind Lou's house. He saw a woman wandering in the field between Lou's cottage and Manfred's Folly. The woman was heading for the cottage.

Shem could see she was sick and needed help. Not being one to interfere with Nature's ways, he waited. He'd learned that lesson long ago. He adored Nature, but he also knew it was relentless and would have its way, according to the Laws of the Cosmos governing Life.

He glanced up at the sky. It was the light blue of late morning before the colors of the day really got down to business. He studied the ground.

He had come to know that every day he was filled inside with dawns and sunlight. Just like the world around him.

Nights filled him with gorgeous stars and purple, distant mysteries waiting behind each black night sky. Just like the world around him.

Suddenly, memories of his mother flooded him. A hard pang of regret shot through him. He fell to his knees. He'd searched for his mother for years, but there was no one left to tell him where she might be by the time he was old enough to go look for her. With anguish, he remembered his mother's thinness and blondness, her paleness, as though life was sucking her dry. She was funny and timid and loved him greatly.

She was unable to tolerate much of life, and he hoped she'd found a good place to live on this Earth, for above all, hers was a Good soul.

Someone interrupted his grief riddled memories. Someone was speaking to him. Urging him to go to the wandering woman and take care of her. Somehow, he suddenly knew the sick woman's name was Mina.

Shem turned and hurried back to camp. Gordon, Timmon, and Lou were sitting around the campfire. How long had he been gone? Time could turn into a weird thing. Was it an instant or an hour? He didn't stop to ask. He was on a mission.

He skidded to a stop in front of them.

"I need to borrow one of the Jeeps. I have to go back to Lou's place to take care of the woman wandering around in the field between the cabin and The Folly. Her name is Mina. Strange name. I never heard it before. I need to go right now!"

Timmon shot to his feet.

"That's my mother's name!"

Shem stared at him silently.

"Who told you to do this?" Timmon shouted.

"You better take my Jeep. It's in better shape."

Gordon's smooth voice interrupted their possible confrontation.

"You're obviously on a time limit, so explanations later, Timmon. Let him go. Follow him."

Gordon tossed the Jeep keys to Shem. Shem grabbed them and turned away. A minute later, he was gone.

Crowell Goforth Restus was Timmon's father. The golden man's time was almost up. The outcome of today lay in the hands of the Walker, his son the Dreamer, and the Forest Whisperer.

Right now, he needed to see the son he had given into the woman's keeping. Only a glimpse, but still, he needed enough to get by on. What was he like? A few seconds later, the campfire flared up as though stirred by a wind. Sparks flew everywhere. Timmon stood by the campfire. Gordon and Lou were takling on the other side of the Jeep. Shem had just left.

Timmon hesitated. He should follow Shem right now, but something held him back. The fire suddenly blazed up, tossing cinders up in a whirling circle. Suddenly, a man stood a few feet away. Startled, Timmon stared at him.

The man was golden-haired. He looked just like himself. Timmon and the man advanced on each other, circling and studying each other.

Timmon swiped his hand across his forehead. It was hot. Maybe the older, golden-haired man in the rich, swaying robes denoting some kind of rank, was some kind of a vision or at least, a dream.

Golden sparks flew around the stranger's head. Then he smiled tenderly at Timmon.

"Change your name to Crowell Goforth Restus the Third, before all of the courts in this land after the woman who birthed you has passed. Time always brings its own forms of justice. After it is done as bespoken, then we meet again."

Timmon and the man stared at each other. A warm pink energy touched Timmons heart tenderly, shooting sparks of gold through it. Then the man vanished.

Timmon reached down and picked up the staff lying on the ground where the golden-haired man had appeared.

It was a beautifully carved, elegant piece of magic work. The staff fit his hand perfectly. A name was carved on its handle. Crowell Goforth Restus the Third. Impulsively, Timmon whirled the cane around to test its balance. It was perfect.

Gordon interrupted him.

"It is urgent that we return to Lou's...ah...abode. Somehow, time has warped...escalated. We'll have to make do with what we already have and know to deal with the evil awaiting us. We must hurry."

A few minutes later, they were packed and on the road.

Dere's a mystery
waitin' in hell
tho' it cain't sing
or ring a bell
it's still dere'
come on, honey
lets git' the hell
outta' here!

Chapter Ten

Shem and Crazy Jack

Shem jerked the jeep to a stop in the cabin driveway. Clouds of dust billowed up behind him. Crazy Jack was nowhere in Sight. Shem jumped out and ran to the back of the cabin.

Crazy Jack stood at the edge of the field, watching a woman stagger across the field between The Folly and the cabin. She was far enough away that Shem couldn't tell anything about her. He started into the field to help her. Crazy Jack stopped him.

"No. Not yet. That woman's dying. You must go barefooted, for one thing," Crazy Jack said.

"And there is more..."

Shem stared at Jack impatiently.

"You're a Walking Philosopher. A Nomad. A Traveler," Crazy Jack said.

"You can't help that woman without being aware of your personal Traveler's philosophy. You've had it hard 'cause you've been forced to walk alone. But your walk has made you stronger than you think.

There are people in our world who end up alone and isolated most of their lifetime. Many see through other people's crap, so they don't like who most other people are. That intense individuation causes separation. Did you ever separate from someone unwillingly?"

"My mother." Shem said, a world of hurt in his voice. "I wonder where she is every day of my life. She told me who my real father was before she left that piece of crap husband that was killing her off with his rutting and laziness."

He shrugged. "She left when I was twelve."

Crazy Jack didn't look at him. Instead, he studied the woman in the field. Then he handed Shem a pair of old time flying goggles.

"I don't know who she is, but you'll need everything you got to handle her. Here, put these on."

Shem, was now barefoot and wearing fitted goggles. A barefoot pilot.

"Bring her here. Somebody is waitin' for her."

Shem stared at Crazy Jack.

"Okay. It may take a while, though. Years, ten minutes, a century. I don't know."

Crazy Jack nodded.

"No problem. We will wait."

Shem took his first cautious step into the magic working in the field.

Beck

Beck was headed for Colorado. Alone. He missed Hattie, although her perpetual insistence on being a simple, forever happy, delightful young girl instead of the grown up woman she really was, frustrated him to the point of no return. Almost. But not quite. He planned to stick around to find out if Hattie ever decided to step into the woman she was. If she ever decided to grow up, Beck yearned to explore the possibilities with her.

Still, he wished yakky, childish Hattie was on the road with him, spouting her usual cheerful, silly nonsense. But she was away visiting with Celia and Lily Jean Bloome. She'd been gone a week when he was ordered to go to Colorado immediately. He was told that time was of the essence. That timing was everything in this situation. No one told him what the situation was, though he asked.

Alone on the road, headed for Colorado, with time on his hands and no one to distract him, Beck had time to think.

He was remembering his past. His childhood had been bad, very bad. He hoped that since evil is drawn to evil, just as good is drawn to good,

things must have moved in and things must
have moved out of that little town down south
where he survived his childhood.

The wise brujas of old, the shamans and
healers he'd read, all said the same thing. That
there are positive and negative energy spots on
planet earth that it would serve one well to know
about. Serious places to hang around or to avoid
like the plague. The energies in those places
were polarized in concentrated form to Good or
Evil.

Energy vortexes of all sizes, kinds and
influences were found in houses, jail cells,
everywhere.

Most humans never bothered to research and
find out where the positive and negative energy
areas around them were, or to wonder how those
places might affect them. They just stuck with
the mundane, everyday energies they could see.
As he drove, the memories of his childhood hell
moved in and settled in for a good, long visit.

Beck's mothers

Betty Whitlask, kidnapper and random
murderer, had abducted him when he was a
little kid. He didn't remember quite how old he'd
been. She told him she was his real mother, but
he'd been old enough to remember the soft
goodness of another mother before her. A

mother who fed him sweetness with singing and warm hugs.

Betty Whitlask's father, Beck's only Good grandfather died a miserable death, lasting an eternity out in the shacky old barn on the outskirts of the little, miserable town she'd taken Beck back to. He died because of Beck. That day so long ago, Beck had shoved himself up against the barn outside, listening in horror.

There wasn't a thing he could do to stop her. She'd kill him, too, if he interfered. Her blood lust was up. She'd forced Beck to watch her kill animals with her bare hands before, relishing their fearful whimpers and screams.

The energies changed. Beck was next. Suddenly he knew it. She knew it, too. He heard her laugh from inside the barn. Beck shuddered. She had the Sight. She could get away with almost anything, and she knew it. She wanted to kill him because she'd discovered he had the Sight, too.

"Yoo hoo," she whispered loud enough for him to hear, her sharp, high-pitched voice filled with glee.

"Come on in and watch, honey. You're next. It'll just make it easier for me to catch you."

He'd turned from the barn that day and sneaked hastily back through the tall, hot summer grass, racing past the ugly house, his nerves shot. But he held on and didn't break out into a full run until he was a quarter of a mile or so down the road.

He ran sketchily, breathing hard, making little noises, hiding behind trees and summer roadside growth until the stench of her bloody jubilation was gone.

He ran until he reached the Beamer farm down the road. Beck ran up the driveway and sneaked into the Beamer house. It was noon. Old man Beamer should be eating in the kitchen down the hall. Beck slipped down the hall and into old man Beamer's bedroom. He grabbed the money lying on top of the bureau and stuffed it into his jeans pocket. Old man Beamer's best pocketknife lay beside the money, along with a piece of paper with an address printed in pencil on it.

Beck grabbed the knife and scrap of paper and stuffed them into his pocket. Beck looked around at the peaceful bedroom. Old man Beamer's rocker sat in a corner. Knickknacks and faded photos in frames covered the antique wood furniture. His old cat lay on the floor, taking a noonday nap. Tears misted Becks eyes. He'd basked in the Goodness that poured through old man Beamer's house many times. He left the same way he came, listening to old man Beamer eat his lunch.

Beck stopped running a short distance away from old man Beamer's house. He sighed wearily and turned back. He made his way back to the house and into the kitchen. Old man Beamer was sitting at his table, eating a doughnut from the Tasty Bakery in town. He looked at Beck.

"Thought you was gone. Better hurry."

"Thanks," Beck said. He lunged forward and hugged the old man tightly.

"Git' gone. Fast. No tears. They'll make ye' pay. Go on now. Oh, and don't lose that address."

Beck nodded and ran. He'd lost the paper with the address on it somewhere along the way. He stayed on the run year after year to avoid the Chasers. The Chasers were all Evil Sighted. Their mission in life was to destroy all Sighted people that worked with Goodness.

Betty Whitlask had him put on their list. After he grew up, Beck looked up a history of the little Podunk town he'd run away from. He read that the good grandfather and the closest neighbor, Mr. Benjamin Beamer, had been tortured and murdered by what was assumed to be a cult gang.

Betty Whitlask had disappeared. The cops seemed to think that same cult gang that murdered the two men had abducted her. Beck knew better.

Old man Beamer had known what was coming and died for him. It was as simple as that. There was no greater love. It was then that Beck dedicated his life to serving his gift of

Sight. In time, he had discovered that he was a Tree Whisperer.

His thoughts took another turn.

Where was Betty Whitlask now? He'd tried to find out from time to time, but the Chasers she'd set on him after he ran, never gave him enough time to stop running and get a hold of any roots to hang on to.

No information available, so he could make an informed stand against her. She was still out there somewhere, hunting him down like he was an animal instead of an abducted child she'd done wrong. Betty Whitlask loved the chase. The green poison of Revenge coursed through her veins. A constant outpouring of brutal activities fed its flame, kept it burning.

Suddenly, Beck had enough of remembering the misery he'd endured.

He lurched into a rest stop off the highway near Trinidad, Colorado, and parked. He locked his doors and placed the small, black gun under his seat. Ready to grab. He fell asleep in seconds. Trouble was, he dreamed of her again.

Betty Whitlask

She was crossing the yard towards him. A thin tall woman with red-blond hair, white skin, and pale blue eyes. She'd bragged to him that she hailed back to the Vikings. She said she still liked their ways of killing, plundering, and pillaging.

A terrified little boy of seven, Beck stood rooted to the spot, waiting. He'd traveled down this road before. He knew the evil, crazy bitch was full of new, appalling, stored up stuff to say and do to him.

Fear sped through him as he recognized the telltale signs of her escalating fury. He watched the way she strode toward him with purpose. Each time she punished him, Betty told him parts of her life story, repeating them over and over as though she was in a trance state. Young Beck memorized almost every word each time, concentrating on the words detailing her life instead of on his fear and the pain she was inflicting on him. And, because it might mean his life to remember her words.

She said she'd run her mother off and took over her father and four younger siblings by the time she was seven. Her father was away, flying planes all the time and Betty's four younger siblings, terrified of Betty, minded her. All was well until noticeable violations of so-called sanity on Betty's part arose and were noted over and over.

When there was enough proof, Betty's mother was called home from her life of drugs, men, and extended stays in fancy mental institutions (rest farms), to reign over her children and home once again.

Betty was fifteen when her mother came home. Betty threatened to kill her, so her parents placed her on heavy duty psychiatric meds and flew her to Hawaii. Abused for years and terrified of her, all four of her siblings hoped she'd never return. But instead of staying in Hawaii as they'd hoped, Betty found a husband and got married.

Her husband was a loud, obnoxious Marine, a man stationed temporarily in Hawaii. He knew how to handle crazy, for he lived in his own version of it. The two crazies flew back to the states, married, and moved from Minnesota to Texas to successfully raise four crazy, cruel, obnoxious children.

She told Beck that once upon a time, she had been beautiful and elegant. She'd wanted only the best. A fine husband, four children, a spacious home with a pool, and an A-list of friends over to visit. All of that was hers, too. Fine china, eating a model's diet, until her too tall, too thin, two dimensional, and by now, mean and vicious four children were grown and gone, off tormenting others in ways their parents had taught them.

Always on the edge, alone in the looming, empty house when her husband died a few years later, Betty Whitlask's psychiatrist prescribed more pills to augment Betty's already growing stash of anti-psychotic and other psychiatric meds.

Rambling around in her large, empty nest, no one was left to keep Betty in the country of sane. She quickly went off the rails. They tried to put her in a mental institution. She packed up and ran away from her fancy life. Found a new home in this small town where everyone looked the other way. First she kidnapped her father and installed him in a house in her new Podunk little town. He went along with her. He always had.

Then she "found" Beck, and a couple of others like him, to mother. The others came before him. They were gone now. Beck didn't know where. As time went on, she hinted to him of where they were buried, because they were bad boys.

"Madness has consumed her. Hell is right in her."

That's what her father, his good grandpa that she'd whisked away from his home and made him hide out in the little town, told Beck when she wasn't around. They were both terrified of her.

In his dream, Betty Whitlask cuffed him across the head.

"What the hell do you think you're doing, boy?" she snarled. He gazed up at her, a small boy with dark, straight hair, freckles across his nose, his face dead white with fear.

She leaned down close to study him with goggle-eyed, penetrating blue eyes, her red hair hanging in greasy hanks around her face. Her pupils darkened her eyes to almost black. That was a bad sign. He stiffened, waiting.

"You little bastard!" she hissed. He looked up at her with little boy eyes. Gray or green, depending on his mood, his eyes seemed to take in the world at a glance and give back his Sighted Goodness to it. She hated him for that.

Beck Smith, not his real name, shuddered in his sleep. And dreamed on.

Betty Whitlask had made him watch her sleep countless times. He sat in a hard ladder back wood chair, small beside her bed. Staying as motionless as he could, he stared at her. The clock tick-tocked way. It was the only sound breaking the dull, tense silence. He watched as the golf ball size and smaller, hard round things rose to the surface of her skin but never popped out. They roamed her body while she slept, appearing here and there like different size marbles with lives of their own. The bad things hurt her while she slept. He was glad. She cursed the things. She moaned and shoved them away in her sleep.

They knew, for he watched them disappear and when she was just starting to relax again, they popped up somewhere else. The nasty entities had become bold. They'd begun roaming Betty Whitlask's body both day and night, while she was asleep and awake. By the time he escaped, Betty Whitlask was gone. She was insane. Mad. Gone bad. A walking lunatic. A thing.

Beck whimpered in his sleep. She'd laughed at him and preached about how he was to always take care of her. That was the worst horror of all. Thinking that he'd be tied to her for the rest of her life. A little kid, he'd half assed believed her. He'd watched in horror, then through a sullen dullness that separated him from what he was seeing. Then she killed her father and came after him.

The bad dreams finally left. Beck slept a few hours and woke up. Weary and soul worn, he took a piss in the bathroom, washed up, and drove on.

Hattie

Hattie and Lily Jean Bloome strolled down the beach outside Lily's beach house. They were discussing the different ways Goodness and Evil could use scents to gain an advantage in a battle when it came to houses.

Hattie's was Sighted. Her strongest Gift was her relationship with houses. She was a House Whisperer.

Hattie understood houses. She knew that most houses were lonesome. Most humans could not hear them or understand their language. As soon as a house realized that

Hattie could hear them, they started chattering to her about everything.

Handily, they also told her all about the humans who lived in them long ago and who lived in them now. They knew their roots thoroughly, and owned strong opinions on their humans' behaviors.

Doors slammed when they were angry. Floors waved, and wood chipped off or became soft when they were sad, and Hattie was around. Hattie knew that neglect of houses showed up in many ways. So did happiness or mourning.

Lily Jean Bloome said, "Now that your lessons are over, you'll have to be on your way. There is a house that needs you. Celia will be going with you. She will be helping the outside of the house from a distance as you deal with it. Mind you, Hattie, maintain your objective observer, and don't get caught up in the house's problems."

"Where will you be?" Hattie asked.

Lily Jean Bloome cast her smoky eyes out over the sea.

"Don't worry. I'll be keeping an eye on everyone."

She patted Hattie's shoulder.

"Now, we must go in, and you must pack."

Lily Jean Bloome smiled at Hattie.

"There is a folder on the front seat. It will explain some of The Folly—The Dolly Manfred Mansion's—history to you. Read it on the way to

Colorado. They call it Manfred's Folly these days."

Lily Jean Bloome paused. "Now, be careful. This is an important assignment. You must maintain your equanimity."

"Oh, sure," Hattie answered confidently. Lily Jean Bloome gave Hattie a long, appraising, sideways look of disapproval. Hattie stayed insistently too young in her own mind. A life and death transformation of an evil house and its roots was needed, not a cute little make-over. Would Hattie ever grow up? Lily frowned at Hattie, but Hattie never noticed. *As Usual,* Lily Jean Bloome thought wryly.

Beck

Beck felt the urge to hurry. Somehow, time was of the essence. He sped towards Gitwell, the refrain insistently in his ears.

"No time to waste!"

Beck rocked the Jeep to a stop in front of The Folly. Was he in time for whatever was going to happen? Rain began pattering down. It pounded the top of the Jeep in a bellowing roar. Then it suddenly stopped. His instincts told him that yes, he'd arrived just in time.

Beck ran for the front porch. Then he heard a cry from behind the house and changed directions. He ran around the seemingly endless, vast old house stinking of rotted bad things and hot ashes and skidded to a stop. Off in the distance, trees were in the process of surrounding an old woman. He heard her scream. He ran towards her.

Mina

Mina felt the Shadow trees moving closer. She realized they weren't going to save her. They were going to kill her! She screamed in terror. In her crafty, hazy, terror-filled mind, she had turned to the trees to flee the grim destiny awaiting her at the end of the field.

The trees had almost surrounded her when a man dressed in black plunged into their midst. The man barked out an order in a strange language and the trees backed away. The trees didn't like it, though. Mina could tell. They loomed over the man.

Shem

Barefoot, with goggles on, Shem left Jack's side and began to slowly and carefully cross the field. He headed towards the woman but she changed directions and turned towards the forest.

At the edge of the forest, the trees began surrounding her. Shem stopped. Stood there. Puzzled, he didn't know what to do next. He waited.

Suddenly, a man in black appeared behind the rotting mansion. He raced across the field to the woman, stopped, and barked out orders at the trees. The trees backed off. The man stood there, keeping them under control.

Shem waited until he realized that the man couldn't handle both the trees and the woman. He ran to them, reached her and grabbed ahold of a remnant of her tattered gown, pulled her away from the trees.

Terrified, he tugged her back towards the center of the field. He glanced at the man in black. He was handling the trees like a lion tamer handles a bunch of mean, fierce lions that plan to eat him alive.

The crazed woman he had grabbed on to was moving like a damn snail. But time was of the essence, and she needed to get a move on. In desperation, Shem began talking to the woman, a thing he never did voluntarily with anyone. He found himself saying things he knew deep down, things he'd never consciously thought about. *Oh hell*, he thought. *It didn't matter anyway. The old broad was nuts, and it looked like she was dying, too.* When he talked she moved faster. Just enough to keep him talking.

"Ma'am, keep heading towards the cabin. Your destiny lies there. Don't change directions again. What will be, will be. You've got to accept it. This universe we live in communicates with us in ways some of us know about, and in many ways we don't know about. This looks like one of those times to me. Spirit's the boss, and it's gonna' run this show. I just hope to live through it. You better start worrying about that, too!"

The woman glared at him and shrieked. "I'm lost! Forever!" She clawed at her face with dirty, long nails.

Shem watched her, a wary look on his face.

"You're dirty," he said, swiftly comprehending the problem. "In your soul, too."

He looked her over.

"Everywhere else too, I guess. In your mind and feelings, too."

He peered at her.

"My guess is you like being dirty."

Just then, dark clouds gathered in the sky and rain began pouring down so hard it made Shem gasp.

Shem knew all about this kind of cleansing rain. Some called it being washed in the blood. This had happened to him once before. A long time ago outside a little church, awhile before his mother ran away. She'd held his hands and laughed and they'd danced in the cleansing rain, a blessing sent by angels, she had said.

"Confess your sins!" Shem shouted at the woman. "Or the rain will never stop!"

Mina screamed words, throwing them at him like deadly bullets intended to kill him.

"I hate everything and everybody, and I've killed and tortured and loved every goddamned second of it. No regrets! None! I just want to hate more! I will kill Timmon first and all the rest when I get my hands on them!"

She curved her hands into dirty nailed claws. Shem had never seen such naked hate. He shuddered, but kept his course.

"Come on, old hag! There's more to say, isn't there?"

Mina glared at him.

"They deserved to die!" she said righteously.

"Timmon deserves to die. And more!"

"Who is Timmon to you that you hate him so much?" Shem asked.

She gave him a hard look.

"He's my son. I want to kill you too." She said, conversationally, as though they were talking about the weather. Shem was shaken to the core of his being by her words, but he didn't let her see it.

Finally he said calmly, "You can't kill Timmon or me. You haven't got the energy. For one thing, you're almost dead. Did you know that? It won't be long now," Shem answered himself, almost conversationally.

"I'm guessing the powers that be are keeping you in this state, so you won't know the peace a Good death brings."

She was an evil old devil. Shem thought.

Shem thought of his Good lost mother. Where was she? The rain stopped. Shem urged the woman down the field in the direction of Lou's cottage. She moved forward like a snail.

I don't know what will happen when we get there, but there's nothing else to be done. Shem realized the woman was on a kind of pilgrimage. There was something more guiding her towards a goal. Shem wondered what the goal was. He said gently, "Let's go home."

Shem thought about pilgrimages. He'd been on one for many years. He'd met others who were on pilgrimages, usually going somewhere to worship a religious deity, or for healing purposes.

He'd met a few like himself, lost people looking for a magic sacrament to end their search, to bring them fulfillment, end their suffering. Some of the wanderers were searching for siblings, parents, grandparents, aunts, uncles. Shem was searching for his mother.

Shem glared at the evil, dirty woman. His mother wasn't filthy like this murderous mother was! His mother was frail and clean and Good and soft and-suddenly he realized that she'd been voiceless in her Goodness. Where was she now? There was no doubt that his mother needed his protection. When he got this crazy old bat to her destination, he would no longer put off finding his mother and saving her.

He just wanted this strange ordeal over with. He took a firmer grip on the woman's ragged gown, tugging her along. Shem kept Mina moving toward Crazy Jack and the cabin while Beck held back the hungry forest.

Hattie and Celia

Hattie smiled in delight at the gorgeous, welcoming mansion nestled on a patch of property. Celia was driving. They'd seen the flat field and the forest behind the mansion, and Beck out there, dealing with a bunch of trees. Dismissing Beck, Hattie examined the old mansion with her eyes. It was beautiful! She glanced back at Beck again. She heard him shouting orders at the trees. No problem. He could handle it.

I guess the house is mine to deal with. *That's okay,* Hattie thought. *It had been a long trip. Celia wasn't chatty, as usual, a thing that could have made the time pass much quicker.*

Hattie didn't ask Celia why she was being so short with her. Why she was so grim about everything. Hattie was a person who prided herself on never getting caught up in people's bad moods. And anyway, she was ready to eat a hundred cookies, burnt or not.

She jumped out of the Jeep before Celia could warn her, before Celia came to a full stop. That was because the old mansion smelled like warm, fresh baked cookies with raisins in them. There was a slightly bitter under-scent, but Hattie didn't hesitate as she should have. She chose to think that the peculiar, underlying smell was caused by the raisins. Maybe the baker had burnt some of them.

Hattie ran up the steps and straight at the cozy, warm, welcoming doors of The Folly. Without a second thought, she raced through the wide open doors and into The Folly. The double front doors slammed shut behind her. Hattie didn't care. It was a house. She was a House Whisperer. She could handle it. After she ate cookies. Hattie ran for the kitchen, stubbed her toe on a rug, and fell. She landed beneath the floor in a very odd looking, closed space.

She lay. Still. Very still.

Slowly she realized that the house had tricked her. She sniffed. The cookie smell was gone. This house stunk of bad doings. She sighed. She'd probably have to find out what the problem was. Houses always told her their histories. She was a house therapist, a House Whisperer.

The house held her close in the floating space beneath the floor. Weird. She could see the living room from where she lay. Then the floor coughed and threw her up. She went sprawling across the rug.

"Irish Soda Bread!" Hattie shouted. "You best behave!"

The house became still again. Sheer white curtains bloomed over the windows. A gentle breeze began to move them. Hattie watched them.

"Ha!" she shouted in derision. "Trickster!"

She turned when someone or something opened a door. An ancient victrola in the living room began playing waltz music from an old black and white movie. Hattie didn't know which movie, but it looked like monsters and their kin were dancing in silhouettes on the now shadowed walls of the living room.

"Come here so I can see you," a voice ordered.

"Who are you?"

"Vance Romaine," a steely, hoarse voice answered. "Who's asking?"

Hattie said, "Oops!"

"Come on in. There's only me here, honey. The rest are away on a road trip. I don't bite," Vance Romaine invited in a syrupy voice.

But the rug hugged her close. It wouldn't let go. Suddenly, Celia stood beside her. She stomped on the rug, grabbed Hattie's hand and jerked her free of the rug's grasp.

"Greedy thing!" Hattie shouted impulsively at the rug.

"Irish soda bread!" she shouted again and again as Celia pulled her out the front door and down the porch steps. The Folly released them. The wide double doors slammed shut behind them

"Gordon warned us not to go in," Hattie said ruefully when they were safely away from the house.

Celia said dryly, "Yes. He did say that. And because you never listen, now I have expended certain of my reserves rescuing you."

I'm sorry," Hattie said contritely. "But it smelled so good! Like cookies and grandmas and doilies and aprons."

"Stop!" Celia ordered her. Hattie was wandering toward the monstrous contraption of a house again, blabbing away, not thinking.

Weasel Manor, Celia thought. *Yeah. Let her have it.*

"Oh, to hell with it! You're impossible to teach anything! You don't listen and you never learn. Well, you're on your own now, little kiddo. Little girl. Little darling. Little brat who never grew up!"

Celia turned her back on Hattie and the house and stalked away. Hattie stared after Celia the Amazon. Celia. She was shocked. Beautiful, tall and commanding Celia, her long brown hair a gorgeous waterfall Hattie often envied. Celia had called her names. It finally dawned on Hattie. Celia was mad at her!

Ceila flung more words back over her shoulder.

"And you're a brat! A stupid one at that!"

Hattie was dumbfounded by Celia's words, not realizing the house was drawing her closer and closer again.

Celia turned around. "See, the house is going to suck you back in and destroy you. All over again. You put yourself and everyone around you at risk to keep your cute, young girl image. How old are you, really? Aren't you ever get it?"

The hostility in Celia's voice cut through the air. Hattie stared at Celia. What Celia said was true. Suddenly, she was tired of the front she'd worked so hard to keep up through the years.

"I'm thirty-nine."

Hattie heard herself admitting her true age to Celia. Her true age was her biggest and longest kept secret. Now it was out in the open. She said it over and over. The house listened and mocked her in an ancient voice.

"Thirty-nine! Thirty-nine!"

Hate reeked from it and rippled through the air.

Celia said, "Grow up, Hattie! Lives are at stake here! Beck, who you are supposed to give a damn about, is holding off a fricking Dreadful Forest by himself! You don't give a damn about him, do you? Another man is guiding a very sick woman towards a little cottage. Get your sorry ass in gear. You're not the only one here, you selfish little bitch!"

Hattie took a step back. Stared at Celia.

"You're right. I guess it's time."

Ain't no dead ends allowed here
Ain't no need to weep or pace
For God's grace is hal-lo-wed
An' it's walkin' about dis' ol' place

Chapter Eleven

Celia

Celia was pissed off at Hattie for putting everyone's lives at risk with her denial of how bad evil could be. There was no room in Celia's plans for Hattie's monkey business, her selfish childishness. She didn't need or want naïve, childish Hattie to endanger this mission any longer. Abruptly, she dismissed all thoughts of Hattie. She was on her own now.

She might have to conquer this evil all by herself. Her and Timmon. Celia gusted out an impatient breath. Where the hell was he?

Celia had been waiting for Timmon all her life. She was his. He was hers. That was all there was to it. Sometimes he avoided her, but he wouldn't forever. She would win him over someday. She'd met Timmon at the desert store when he was ten and came to live there.

She heard a vehicle and turned to look at the road. Timmons Jeep. Jubilation rushed through her. She raced towards the Jeep, but it sped on by.

She stopped, puzzled. What the hell was going on? She watched the Jeep pull into the driveway of the little cabin. She watched Timmon jump out of the Jeep. He raced behind the cabin and stopped at the edge of the field. She watched Gordon race after him, stop him, put a hand on his arm.

She watched Timmon drop his head to his chest in defeat.

Then a miracle began. In amazement, Celia watched as a halo of sparks formed around Timmon's golden haired head. Tears filled her eyes. Timmon was her beloved. Something amazing was going on here.

Suddenly Hattie stood beside her.

"I need to go back and deal with the house."

Hattie spoke to Celia in a grownup voice.

"Whatever!" Celia snarled.

"Just get the hell away from me!"

Hattie fastened her eyes on Celia. She had watched Celia when the jeep drove by without stopping. At the look on Celia's face, Hattie finally realized the depth of Celia's love for Timmon. And then there was Beck. Was he okay?

A new sense of urgency filled her. Hattie swayed, swiftly sorting and assimilating her newfound discoveries of who she really was.

The house was whispering to her. Time to get it done. She began whispering back to the house. "Okay!" she said to Celia, who angrily ignored her.

This time, Hattie was cautious. She was no longer the naïve kid who'd ran straight into the house. Lightning fast changes were taking place.

This time, Hattie would stay aware and mind her manners. Do things properly, this time. She took a deep breath and climbed the steps to the house. Inside, she sat down in an antique chair like a little girl in a flouncy dress, waiting to take tea with her favorite and most beloved grandma. She began entrancing the house. The house couldn't resist her good manners.

"Tell me your story," Hattie urged the house. "I really, really, really, want to know all about you. I know you are old and have many interesting facets. Tell me, who were the architects of your beginnings? And are you planning any renovations in the near future? You must be a little bit bored of the same old thing. You know, hate, hate, and more hate. And all the evil junk that goes with it, like decay, stenches, dry rot and slipping gables. Stuff like that."

The house answered Hattie.

"Almost all parts of us now belong to Dolly Manfred's hate. Dolly Manfred was a sick woman. She had a bent soul. She planted her pathological, deep-seated hate and grudges into the heart of this place. We didn't like it. But we had to do what she wanted, as she was our owner. We became evil, and we became trapped. All of us. Rugs, china, walls, doors, people. You name it."

The house spoke matter-of-factly to Hattie.

"People get trapped, too, if they stay here. Only the ones who have closed the doors to their Goodness and given in to Evil are allowed inside. It has been this way since Dolly Manfred was jilted by her lover and took revenge on him."

"What did she do to him? Who was he? Who was she? How long ago did this happen?"

"If you keep rushing us, we won't tell you anything," the house answered huffily.

"Sorry," Hattie said.

"She murdered him here. Stabbed him. In the basement. It was once upon a time, long, long ago..." the house sing-songed.

Celia heard a door slam at the back of the house. She raced around the house to the field and got there just in time to see a man run out of the back door of The Folly. He ran across the field towards the man leading the sick woman at a snail's pace towards the cabin. They had their backs to him.

Celia glanced at Beck. His back was to the two in the field. He was busy fending the Dreadful Trees off. He had his hands full and couldn't help.

She glared at Crazy Jack, Timmon, and Gordon. They stood at the field edge by the cabin, waiting. Surely they could see the running man? What were they waiting for?

Celia watched the man raise his hand when he reached the woman and man in the field. He held a long knife in it.

He quickly overtook the couple, jerked the woman around, and stabbed her through the heart. He released her and she fell to the ground. Quickly, he stabbed himself in the heart and fell. It was over before anyone could stop him.

Celia heard a shout. It was Timmon.

"No! Mother!" he shouted.

He started to run across the field. Gordon and Crazy Jack grabbed Timmon and held him back. Timmon struggled to throw off both Gordon and Jack's grip on him.

Shem

Shem staggered and almost fell as the man shoved him away from Mina and grabbed the woman. Stunned, Shem watched the man stab her, then himself.

In shock, Shem bent over and picked the woman up in his arms. His only thoughts were to protect her. He had to save her. He had to save his mother. But she was gone. And he knew it. The woman weighed nothing. She was as light as though she'd been a feather he'd just found lying on the ground.

He took up the journey they had undertaken together, carrying her, walking slowly across the field to Timmon.

Now he knew why he was barefoot and wearing goggles. His mother was gone. She was in a higher place. A place where hot air balloons and small, two person planes buzzed the clouds.

He heard chanting begin around him. Voices that sprang up from the Earth. Voices that urged him to keep walking when he faltered. He knew that all of this happening was in Spirit's keeping now. Her and him and all of them.

Gordon and Jack held on to Timmon. They waited at the edge of the field. Nothing Celia was seeing made any sense to her. When things didn't make sense, Celia always took action. She became an arrow aimed at her target. She ran for Timmon. But some kind of time warp held her back. She felt like she was wading through layers of shuffling legal papers and fading legal announcements as she slowed down and stumbled along. When she slowed to a fast walk, the words began making sense. Someone was speaking Hallowed Words pertaining to Covenants and Earth's Mastery of Matter and the Laws of its Dispersal. The Laws of the Mother.

She knew Timmon was hearing the same words. The Laws of the Mother's Covenant with the Earth were resounding, echoing all across the field.

Celia stopped. She looked across the field at Timmon. This wasn't hers to handle. She turned and headed back to The Folly. The way was clear and bright and empty. She began to run. She rounded the corner of The Folly. Hattie was standing outside. The house was just finishing its story to Hattie.

"About time!" Hattie snapped at Celia. She pointed her finger to the battered old hippie bus and the load of Vance Romaine followers trapped inside the bus parked behind her.

Angry and shouting, Vance's people were straining to get through the invisible wall Hattie had put up to keep them from leaving the bus.

"I can't keep the shields up and deal with the house too! Tell them to get in their vehicles and get the hell out of here, or they will die...or at least come to great harm!"

She put her hand down. The invisible wall collapsed. Vance's minions rushed forward.

Suddenly, an old, white haired woman stood beside Celia, a gold watch in her hand. She moved something on the watch, and Vance's minions slowed down, then stopped.

"I'm Louise Hope Cornfield. Nice to meet you," she said conversationally, to Celia and Hattie, as though they had all the time in the world.

"Now, let me adjust the time warp for these…brats…before I hand the watch to you, girl-woman. After all, this is Timmon's ancestral home. His mother is ending her life here, too, like her ancestor, Dolly Manfred. The knife Dolly Manfred killed with has now killed the evil ancestor that arose to take her place."

Celia stared at the woman in horror.

"Karma." Lou answered the look and shrugged.

Hattie, Vance's minions, and the house stood still, frozen in time. Celia stared at the watch in the woman's hand.

"How?" she asked.

Lou said, "Later… I will explain…if the watch is still here. It might not be. Who the hell knows?"

With Lou's swear words, Celia's confusion stopped. She knew exactly what to do now. She whirled around and glared at Vance's minions. Everything unfroze. Time moved again.

"Get your pint sized evil asses out back and into your vehicles! Get the hell out of here, and don't come back! Ever. You listen and do it quick or die! It's your choice. Get going!"

Celia began swinging the silver sword with gold handles that suddenly appeared in her hands. Vance's followers unfroze and raced to the bus and their other vehicles.

Lou strolled over to Hattie and placed the magic watch gently in Hattie's hands.

"Help the house. Go ahead."

"How do I use it?" Hattie asked.

"You hold it like you're doing right now. Walk through the house slowly, but don't go near the basement. This watch will remove the curses of each age this house has endured, and re-set its age and Good magic. It is a gift to the house, because in its beginning, it was a truly magical, Good place. Go on now. Hurry!" Lou urged.

"Pumpkin soup!" Hattie yelled as she raced up the porch steps and into the house.

Lou shook her head as she watched Hattie run up the steps. Some magicians stay young forever. Maybe it was supposed to be that way.

"Everybody is going through changes."

Lou muttered. Just as her words ended, Lou began shedding things...extra wrinkles, the old Crone's shawl she was wrapped in. She looked down at her feet. Her shoes were changing. No more ugly brown clodhoppers. Her slender feet became encased in lovely tan sandals. Her toenails a pretty pink. She expected to tremble in fear because she was being seen, but Mr. Fear didn't show up. For the first time, Lou stopped chasing Mr. Fear. Because Gordon was here. She sighed and gave up and gave in. She wanted him more than she wanted Mr. Fear. She wanted ever so much for Gordon to see her like this. Her proper age, and all pretty. She wasn't young, but neither was Gordon. It was good.

She heard Hattie shouting inside The Folly. She watched Vance's minions drive past Celia single file, sedately. Once they reached the little lane, they were off like lighting with engines roaring. In a very short time, they were all gone. Celia laid down the sword and strolled over to Lou. Lou examined her with her eyes. This one wasn't even sweating. She was rosy and full of Light, ready to do battle again.

"I like your new look," Celia said, examining Lou's pink nails, sandals, new dress.

"Thanks."

"Did you place no memory of this place in each evil one's memories?"

"I did," Celia answered.

"Good."

They turned to The Folly where Hattie was shouting, "Apple pie!"

Lou and Celia grinned at each other. Lou said wryly, "I believe we are witnessing a historic moment in the time frame continuum."

They climbed the steps and went into the house. Nothing tried to stop them. Hattie was standing in the middle of the drawing room.

"Pineapple sugar!" Hattie exclaimed.

"It's time for me to take back the watch." Lou stated.

Watch in hand, Louise Hope Cornfield spoke to the house in the High Speech she'd only used twice before. Her tone shook the house and it listened, a thing it wasn't fond of doing.

"The logic of the human world is more limited than that of the universe and all its powers! Be still, house, and obey your destiny, or you might become a tiny, one room cottage on a steep slope on a mountain top where no one ever goes! Or maybe a hovel in the back streets of a large, dirty medieval city...or a tenement in New York City in its beginning. If you would like a better choice, then listen."

"Celia. Hattie. Come here."

They gathered around her until they made a circle. Lou turned the gold stem with the notched flat knob. The indentations clicked loudly in the room.

"There isn't much time left. Here is learning, for you will need to have it while you change. Survival dividends belong to the noon hour. All Good is boring. We have to have Dark challenges and overcome them. If we don't overcome them, they take us down to midnight with their buildup and hold us there, like what happened to you."

She turned the watch to 6 p.m. "Detecting evil or witnessing evil. Willful malice. Don't join in ever again!"

A door opened and closed. Gordon stood beside Lou.

"May I?"

He smiled down at her and gently took the gold watch from her hands. He turned to Celia and Hattie.

"Go to Beck. He needs your help. Lou and I will finish this."

They left, and Gordon and Lou turned to the house. Gordon scolded the house.

"No more nonsense, Manfred's Folly! No more choice. You have welcomed every guest that ever came under your roof with the best you could offer, whether it was maligning Light or Evil doing Dark or praising Light or Dark. That's over. Now, you are on your own. Become yourself. Re-build yourself and stand up for Good!"

Gordon commanded. He tapped the gold watch in his hand.

"Destiny has informed me that you have only twenty-one hours and ten minutes left to make any changes you may wish to. Just know that you cannot remain as you are, or we will burn you down to the soil. Dolly Manfred and her history has to be erased from this negative energy vortex. No more sheltering her generations in the basement either. You're not very good with them. No more towering over things, either."

The house began muttering and darkening. It was not happy. Lightning zigzagged through the rooms. Gordon grabbed Lou's hand in his and hurried out of the house. He closed the front door behind them, and led Lou down the steps. When they were a good distance away from the house, he stopped and looked her over.

"You've changed. I like it. Pretty dress- and hair."

Lou blushed. Behind them, Manfred's Folly set to work.

Beck

Beck was exhausted. The trees tripped him, tossing him into the dirt again.

"We like being part of a haunted forest!" the trees shouted, branches dangling and cracking, tossing leaves, mounding them over Beck.

Beck struggled to his feet just as Celia and Hattie appeared beside him.

"Giving you a run for your magic?" Celia joked. Hattie grinned.

The trees closest to Beck surrounded the three of them.

Hattie spoke to the trees.

"Okay, trees, just so you know, we are women. Females. We understand where you're coming from better than any man ever could. Men don't understand that you might like a community in which you can grow saplings, in which you can cherish acorns, pecans, and all manner of other nuts."

Hattie's voice was soft and wheedling. Beck stared at her.

A tree nickered and shed a few leaves. "That was a play on words, but oh, so true," it said.

"And fruit. You must miss the fruit trees and their ability to mist the air with fragrances and to bear fruit children. See, it's a woman thing, isn't it?" Hattie added, watching Beck. A different tree let out a short sob, then quieted.

Hattie said, "Yeah. And then you want to live with all age trees. In a tree community where Saplings on up to Elders live. But who can do that when you've been steeped in black, ugly magic by a bunch of humans wanting to do everything harm, including trees? I mean, if you'd gone against them, you'd have been firewood!"

Beck listened, astonished as Celia said, "They are all gone now and will never be able to return. We have seen to that. So, you are free now."

"Really?" Beck asked.

"Yes. Really."

Celia gave Beck a "Shut up, stupid!" look.

"Except for one," Celia added, putting a finger to her lips to shush Hattie and Beck.

"Who is it?" a tree asked.

Celia said, "I don't know. He's dead, though. That's his body in the field."

The trees didn't answer. They began to move slowly toward the field. Birds of prey began flocking into their treetops. Beck, Hattie, and Celia backed carefully away from the trees, then turned and ran back to The Folly. It was already beginning to show signs of change. Weird noises were coming out of it, and it shuddered every now and then. Gordon and Lou were waiting for them, standing at a safe distance in the lane in front of The Folly. Gordon shouted to Beck.

"Beck. Go. Go get the woman in the field. Carry her the rest of the way to Timmon. Hurry!"

Beck, used to taking orders from his training with Gordon, hesitated and sent Gordon a strained look.

"You have what it takes to do this," Gordon shouted. "Go!"

Beck turned and ran across the field. They watched him take the woman from Shem's arms and start walking. Shem fell in behind Beck.

Gordon, Lou, Hattie, and Celia walked to Lou's cabin. Part way there, they watched a flock of predatory birds leave the trees branches and descend on something lying in the field. They heard shrieks and screams. They shuddered and looked at each other, looked away, and let it be.

Shem

Shem nestled the woman in his arms, walked at snail's pace towards Timmon. He had to finish this before giving her to Timmon.

"I'm taking you home, Mom." Shem murmured. "To the place you've always belonged. A place where roots are sweet and strong, with no lazy fornicating man anywhere near you to cause you to run away from life again. You'll be happy there." he assured her.

Shem pictured his mother resting in a meadow filled with flowers, the sun shining, the wind dancing over her. She'd been gone a long time. He knew now that he didn't have to search for her anymore. She was already home in a place where love abounded. He had to put his stored up lost mother love some place, so he poured it out over the woman he was carrying. Showered it over her, and it lit up and rang with joy and love.

Then Beck showed up.

"Give her to me, please." Beck said. "Gordon said for me to carry her now."

Shem's heart lightened. His back straightened. His soul sighed with relief. Now maybe he could live a different life. Shem was glad, for he needed his burden lightened. The woman was heavy. He realized that he was giving away the greatest burden he'd ever carried. His broken, wandering heart that had searched for his mother for many weary, long years, finally knew without a doubt that she was at rest somewhere, in peace somewhere, someplace. It was over. He didn't have to search anymore. He looked down at his bare feet with love.

Beck

Beck took the limp woman in his arms and glared down at her with deep loathing. Why had Gordon ordered him do this?

The monster he was holding in his arms didn't weigh much more than a feather. The woman's story was etched on her evil, haggard face. Beck couldn't stand to look at the evil bitch in his arms any longer. He just had to do his duty. He would do what Gordon had asked of him. He looked straight ahead as he walked.

He walked slower and slower without realizing it. The woman got heavier with each step he took. He began to stagger along under her weight.

Suddenly the memories of Betty Whitlask he'd tried so hard to blank out roared into his mind and filled his guts. Fear, pain, and rage rose in him. He glared down at the woman. He held the equivalent of Betty Whitlask in his arms! Rage built in him. He let it have its way.

He shouted at the evil mother in his arms. He shouted all the things he'd been forced to hold back since he was a child stolen from its dear mother by that insane, evil bitch, Betty Whitlask. He thought the shouting would never end, but it emptied itself out. All that was left were just facts. Emotional facts. Betty whitlask was dead. And he'd got to end it with her by carrying this dead woman.

A sweet emptiness filled him. In the sweet emptiness was the absolute certainty that Betty Whitlask was dead. No matter how evil she'd been, Spirit ran her show, too. And her karma, her comeuppance, lay in Spirit's hands.

He was thankful that she'd been human enough to die. The greatest relief he'd ever known seeped into him. He wept with relief.

"Oh mother, where are you? I've got to find you!" he shouted, shaking with revelation and a new purpose. There was no one to stop him finding the mother his abduction had left behind now. He couldn't before, for he might her life in danger, too. But Whitlask and the Chasers were gone. It was time. Maybe he had a father, too. Maybe brothers and sisters. Aunts. Uncles.

The strength of a giant poured into Beck as he took the last few steps and stood in front of Timmon. He knew who this woman belonged to. And it wasn't him. His mother was waiting, somewhere, for her abducted son to come home. Beck handed the feather-weight woman over into Timmon's arms and stepped away. It was over. He didn't have to run away anymore.

Timmon and Crazy Jack.

Timmon took his mother from Shem's arms. He laid her gently down in the grass, and knelt beside her. He studied her gaunt, dark face. Hers was a weary, tired out face that had seen too much suffering. An old face. One he didn't recognize anymore. There was nothing he could do for her. She was dead. His eyes traveled her body. She was thin and frail, not strong and rounded and plump like she'd been when he was a boy. He remembered how she'd grown to hate him, beginning when he was little boy. Why? She'd been afraid of him ever since he could remember. So many questions and no answers.

But Timmon's soul refused to let it go. It raced back through time, putting together pieces of the long lost puzzle for him.

The golden man that appeared out of nowhere a short time ago. He looked just like that man. His mind lingered over the man's words. "Change your name to Crowell Goforth Restus the Third."

Those ere his real father's words. Now he knew why he'd never been able to feel any affection whatsoever for his evil father or his evil father's sons. He traced his mother's face gently in gratitude while the puzzle came together.

"Thank you, Mother, for your gift. You've set me free."

He stood up and looked at Crazy Jack. "You'll do," he said to Crazy Jack and went into his arms sobbing with relief, joy, love, grief. Crazy Jack held him awhile, then pushed him away and examined him with a Sage's eyes.

"You know where you got that funny lookin' cane from, boy?" Crazy Jack asked him.

Timmon didn't hesitate.

"My father."

Crazy Jack grinned.

"That's the correct answer. I knew him, you know."

"Tell me about him," Timmon demanded.

"Not now. Another time," Crazy Jack answered. "You got business to take care of."

By then, Lou, Gordon, Celia, and Hattie were standing near Shem, Beck, Crazy Jack, and Timmon. They all stared at each other, waiting. What to do next?

Lou took charge.

"Shem and Beck, bring that couch from behind the curtain in the cabin out here. It's for your mother to rest on, Timmon. Until we figure out what's next. She deserves that much for what she's done for you boys."

Shem and Beck carried the couch out and set it on the edge of the field facing The Folly.

Timmon picked his mother up and gently placed her on the couch. Lou went inside the cabin and brought out an old-fashioned quilt. One made for a certain child. Made back in West Virginia by the mother of fourteen children a long time ago. A mother who had lost her daughter to rape, to the violence of a darker older time and way. It had been given to Lou by that mother. Lou had saved it for this very day. She'd stored it along with Granny Parse's seeds.

She'd carried everywhere for years, and had never given up on finding the daughter to whom it belonged. Lou laid the lovely homemade quilt over Mina.

"Timmon, this quilt was made by Mina's mother. She wanted me to find her daughter and give it to her. She said Mina was a lovely child."

Timmon said, "I found out just recently that Manfred's Folly was built by one of my great-how many times back-who knows?-grandfather as a gift for that great grandmother. They did well together. The matriarchal lineage passed down Manfred's Mansion lasted until it reached Dolly Manfred. She was a very emotional person, and in a fit of jealous passion, murdered her lover and then killed herself in the basement of Manfred's Folly. She may have killed others, too. I don't know. Her violent act began drawing evil to The Folly. From then on, the place was haunted and eventually got nicknamed The Folly.

My mother, whom I'm pretty sure didn't know this place was a part of our ancestry, was somehow guided here to die. That's what I believe. That's why I'm glad Lou turned the couch to face The Folly. And the quilt- I will always thank you for it, Lou."

Oh, dem' golden shoes
gonna' wear off their spark
if you dances
too much after dark

Chapter Twelve

They decided to build up Lou's campfire and pitch tents. They cooked over the campfire using supplies from Lou's kitchen.

No one ate much. Shem, Celia, Hattie, Beck slept outside with Timmon. Crazy Jack, Lou and Gordon bunked in the cabin. The young people stayed up late. Timmon and Celia reminisced about growing up around Cowboy Johnson's campfires during their desert store years.

Finally, the talk ended. All became quiet around the campfire. Each one lay fast asleep in their sleeping bags. The fire flickered out after a while, and all lay silent. They slept through the whispering and the movements of things in the dark.

The next morning, they gathered inside for breakfast. When it was over and the dishes washed and put away and everything they could think of had been done, they sat down at the table and waited. What to do next was Timmon's call.

Timmon went outside. They all silently followed. He went to the edge of the field where the couch sat facing the field. The quilt lay neatly folded over the back of the couch. He put his hand on it, then peered over it. He froze, his back to them.

"What's wrong?" Celia shouted. She flew to his side.

"She's gone." Timmon announced in a stunned voice. An amazed silence fell. No one knew what to think or to say.

"I bet the trees took her," Lou finally announced. "And I don't want to live here anymore. I've had enough of this place."

Everyone went to the couch to look. Pieces of bark, twigs, moss, and old leaves were all that was left on it. A trail of them led across the field into the Dreadful forest behind The Folly.

Crazy Jack murmured, "Must have happened in the night when we were resting." Forces beyond their Sight or reckoning had been at work.

Timmon picked up the quilt. Beck laid a hand on Timmon's shoulder.

"I need to tell you something. Thank you for letting me help carry your mother to you. Spirit looks out for us in ways that we might not understand when we've stood enough. While I was carrying her to you, I relived my grim childhood. The awful pieces of it fell away while I car Shem stepped over to Crazy Jack who was nodding like crazy.

ried her. Whether she was a good or bad mother, doesn't change the gift she gave me while I held her. While I was carrying her, I changed. I knew things I hadn't known before. My holding her became a voyage of discovery."

Beck added, "When I was a kid, I was abducted from my home by an evil woman. I ran away from her before she could kill me. That evil entity and her evil minions have chased after me all my life trying to find me and kill me. I don't know how it came about while I carried her, but now I know in my soul that that evil woman is dead. And has been for a while. And her minions have been called off. Other fish to fry. Carrying your mother set me free. Now I am free to live and thrive in this world. I thank her for that."

Beck dropped his hand and stepped back. Beck dropped his hand and stepped back.

Tears stood in Timmon's eyes. Shem placed his hand on Timmon's other shoulder.

"I'll have my say, too. Though I usually keep my mouth shut. Your mother set me free, too. I don't need to search for my sweet, ailing, lost mother anymore. She ran away to save her life when I was twelve. She couldn't take me with her. Nobody would take me in. I hunted for her all my life. I don't have to search any more. I know that now because of your mother's death.

My mother is in a better place. A higher place where hot air balloons and planes fly."

Shem stepped over to Crazy Jack who was nodding like crazy.

"Now about my new father. I got one, too Timmon. It's Crazy Jack. He gave me the goggles and told me to go barefoot into the field. He already knew what I didn't."

Celia laid her head against Timmon's back. She circled his waist with her arms and hands.

She said softly. "My mother is Good. But she can never make a decision. That's where evil traps her and holds her hostage. Nothing to be done about that. Not yet.

Your mother returned three souls held in painful hostage to evil since their childhood back to them in the last minutes of her life. Souls are a big deal. They are the oldest part of ourselves and have memories clear back to god knows when. She did it in spite of herself. She didn't want to do it. That was clear. But somehow, Spirit and her higher self intervened.

You and Shem and Beck are the three guys. The three boys. I would like to think that she might have known of the Good she was doing in her last few minutes."

Lou nodded.

"She didn't know what was going on, but I bet her soul knew. Wherever it carried her to, it left with less regrets because you three boys got what your souls needed.

Your mother was washed clean of entities, her hair was untangled and cleaned. Her skin healed and she became lovely in soul and body. She no longer has to live in the Shadows of insanity, to fear the terror of selfish Evil. It is my opinion that you three boys helped her redeem her own soul, too just as she redeemed yours. Whether that's true or not, let's just go with it."

She pointed to Timmon, Shem, and Beck.

"I will say, though, that she ran a little late, waitin' 'til the last minute to do it." Lou said tartly.

Crazy Jack said softly, "Ain't that the truth."

Beck said, "I'm a tree Whisperer. Trees and I have an affinity. I talk to them. They talk to me. They can do things you've never dreamed of. Their spirituality is grand. Did you notice that Vance Romaine's body is gone, too? That the birds took him? Your mother and Vance Romaine no longer had the human souls they were born with at their demise. Their souls were abducted when they were too young to do anything about it. I think the trees have taken those two empty souls dedicated to evil away, and if you let them keep them, that forest of trees..."

He pointed at the dark forest lurking behind Manfred's Folly.

"They will, in time, remove their two worn out souls and replace them with a different kind of soul. It will be done with permission from Nature and the star paths that watch from above. Their souls won't be human souls, but they will be satisfactory.

I will talk to them if you like, Timmon, and try to get the bodies back if you have unfinished business with them. But their souls are already elsewhere. Gone. I suspect the Druids and other Beings that live in that forest have already taken care of the two of them."

Shem said, "Maybe your mother was on walkabout, Timmon. Maybe time as we know it became warped when she began her long, final journey across the field. I don't know how long she was out in Nature, but it was kind to her. It washed her hair clean, and she began to turn pink instead of...anyway, she was remembering the Good little bits of her childhood."

It was up to Timmon now. They waited in silence for his decision.

"Well," Timmon finally said, "let's leave them all to finish out their destinies."

There was nothing more to be said. They gathered around Timmon and solemnly walked down the road to The Folly. Their somber mood lifted as they stood together on the edge of the dusty little lane, watching what was happening to the Folly, going no further in. It was not theirs to do anymore.

The Folly, as it once stood, evil and looming, was gone.

They studied the one-story edifice on stilts standing in front of them. There was no basement under it. The ground underneath it was clean and fresh.

They laughed behind their hands. The small house on stilts looked like someone stayed drunk on rum while forced to live alone on an island. Someone loose with a hammer and a few nails. There were three kinds of bright paint on the outside and shutters everywhere, some of them hanging by a hinge. A very large and menacing black and white "No trespassing!" sign stood in the front yard.

Beneath the large black letters were smaller black letters stating "Beware!" and warning any trespassers that this was an active site for overseeing certain types of architectural procedures that would not stand for any interference whatsoever. The sounds of hammering, shouting, and cursing came from inside the odd-looking dwelling.

Celia giggled, breaking their silence.

"I guess the Folly is declaring its independence!"

"You realize the Folly is going to have to burn down at some point, don't you, Timmon?" Gordon asked.

"Not today, though," Timmon said. Enough was enough.

He looked at those gathered around him affectionately. It would soon be time to bid them all farewell. He would do as the golden-haired stranger-his father- had instructed.

"By the way, I'm changing my name to my real father's name in all the courts I am a part of. I shall no longer be Timmon, son of Mina. I shall be Crowell Goforth Restus the Third."

He grinned at them.

"I haven't come up with a shorter version of that name yet. But I'm no longer a little boy. Any nickname will have to be a man's proper name."

There was a long silence. They all stared at him. He stared back.

Shem spoke up.

"Ummmm...well, me and Beck will have to have new names, too. We're not little boys anymore, either."

A silence fell while they all thought the new situation over. Then Shem said awkwardly, "Thanks to your mother, Timmon...and to whoever you are now."

The three young men shook their heads in agreement, acknowledging Mina's gift to them as they felt the chains of long-ago commitments fall away from them. They each owned their own karma now. A gift was given to each of them by the dying woman. A gift that would affect all of them, not just the three young men.

Shem said, "I know this sounds crazy, but I just had a name come to me. My new name might be Exavier Jones."

He turned in a circle, held out his arms.

"The name has something to do with children. An orphanage? I think I will be staying with Jack until it is time for me to travel to... New Mexico?"

He grinned at Jack.

"No problem." Jack said.

They left The Folly to its renovation efforts, and strolled back to Lou's cabin.

Timmon asked, "Would you like to visit my new property? It's just down the road from here. I think Manfred's Folly will be coming into my keeping, as it is part of my family legacy. But for now, until further notice, I'll stay away. My new land is just down the lane, and well, I'd like you all to see it, walk it with me, and tell me what you think should be done with it."

"I'll look out for the cabin whenever you're away from here," Crazy Jack said.

"You will have to do more than that," Timmon said. "You'll need to be elected the mayor of Gitwell so you can change the name of the town and get rid of the negative influences still being drawn there."

Crazy Jack stared at Timmon. After a while, he said, "What's the pay for a job like that?"

They grinned at each other.

"Whatever you want," Timmon answered.

"Here's why I need you to do the job. It's an awfully big job. The job requires skill, knowledge, and guts. Evil likes to follow the same energy trails and deepen them, so it has more darkness to hide in. Jack, you're the best man for the job, for you know all about the evil dwelling in Gitwell. The history of Gitwell has to be removed from all memory so none of the entities or persons that live there, ever remember Manfred's Folly or the old town's name."

Crazy Jack studied the ground while everyone waited. In a few minutes he answered Timmon. "Leave it to me. But I have to do it my own way. Time wise and in all other ways. Understood and okayed? And I'll be well paid, too. Probably a rich man by the time it's over."

Crazy Jack paused, then grinned.

"Also, no one will remember my old name, either. It's best that way for the same reasons. I would like to not carry that burden the rest of the time I have left on this Earth."

"Yes, Jack. It's a deal."

Timmon added, "I think I shall try to find my real father."

"Jack, Shem will help you," Lou interrupted. She turned to Shem. He was staring at her, a surprised look on his face.

"How did you know?" he asked.

"That you have the Sight and no place to live or put down roots and thrive?" Lou smiled. "That you want to stay here? The cabin is yours, Shem. I'm gonna' deed it to you. Hook, line, and sinker.

You go to Illinois when the time comes and take care of your personal business, and your home will be right here waiting for you.”

“What are you planning to do? Where will you go?” Shem asked Lou. Lou went to Gordon and stood beside him. She waited. Finally, he took her cue.

“I...ahh..ahem...”

Timmon snickered, then broke into laughter. He’d never seen Gordon caught off guard before. Never, ever. “Ha ha!” Timmon laughed. The rest laughed, too.

When the laughter died down, Gordon glared at all of them, composed himself, and said in an offended tone,

“That’s enough out of all of you. Here’s how it really is.” He paused for effect. “And has been for quite some time.”

Dramatically he rose to his fullest height, swept Lou backward, looming over her until she was dangling in his arms, looking up at him with eyes like saucers.

Daring her to look away, he said, his handsome dark eyes riveted on hers, “Lou’s home is with me. We are going to be partners in many new adventures, aren’t we, Lou?”

She nodded helplessly.

He let her go. She swayed upright.

“Partners, mister! And don’t ever think of bendin’ me over like that agin’! Why, I like to a’ got whiplash from it!” Lou complained, rearranging her clothes. Gordon blushed and looked embarrassed. The whole group looked at him in astonishment. Suave Master of Mime Gordon was never embarrassed!

In an instant, Lou realized what her careless words had done to him. Hastily she said, "It's jist' that you're the finest, handsomest man I ever met, and I want our personal doin's to be a little more private."

Gordon still pouted, face flushed.

"You are the handsomest man in these here parts!" Lou said again.

Why, you're prettier than Timmon...and Shem...and..."

"We get the message," Timmon interrupted. They all laughed. There was nothing like a little comic relief to let a bad moment go. Spontaneously the group lined up to hug Lou. They would have hugged Gordon too, but he was against it. Instead, they grabbed Lou and hugged her while Gordon supervised.

"Not too tight. Let her breathe, okay?"

When they finished hugging her, Lou turned to Gordon.

"Only one more name to change."

"Whose?" Gordon asked.

'Well, that bunch ain't the only ones needin' a nice name change. I might need a purty' new name..."

Lou sent Gordon a long, appraising look. Gordon flushed again and looked away.

Everyone began laughing while Gordon posed, wiggled an eyebrow and smirked down at Lou, who he was holding possessively in the crook of one arm.

"How about we all retire to my place in Boulder? It has a spa, among many other exceptional accoutrements. We could all rest up again and make our new plans."

He smiled down at Lou again. She blushed and gave him another long look. Then she snapped out defensive words, "Shem and Jack can move into the cabin. Shem has learned to milk Bessie. Jack can keep an eye on both of Timmon's properties."

Gordon snickered and looked at the others helplessly.

"She'll probably always have to have the last word."

"You first." Lou said.

The beginning of a new plan was in place. Relieved, they agreed. Boulder, it was. Timmon, suddenly lighthearted and swept free of every burden, gave Celia a long, deep, appraising look. She blushed.

He said, "Yes. I think you and I spending more time together is appropriate, given that we have to make plans for a possible church or maybe a desert store on my new property."

Celia stared at him in astonishment. Hope and wonder filled her face. She strode to him and threw her arms around him and held on like she would never let go. Timmon held her close. Soft light surrounded them.

Just then, Hattie sidled over to Beck and impulsively kissed him on the neck. He drew back in astonishment and stared at her. She met his examination of who she was with a woman's measure. She didn't bat her eyes at him or act silly, as she'd always done before. She stood still and waited, sure of his prognosis. She was correct.

"You're not a little brat any longer, are you?" Beck stated.

"Sometimes. But only when I need to be." Hattie answered. Beck pulled her into his arms and kissed her thoroughly. She gladly let him.

"Whew! Is it hot today, or is it just me?" Beck said, stepping away from Hattie and fanning himself. Everyone laughed.

Life had given three of them one of the most precious gifts it held. Redemption through the intercession of a mother. They were loved and now were able to love again. To go forward holding love's hand.

Good or bad, in the giving, the lives of the men and women would be blessed or maybe cursed, and many others, by the unknown woman once named Mina, mother of a man once named Timmon. The generations would continue to forward their own legacy. Timmon's legacy.

Remember, not all those who wander are lost.
J.R.R. Tolkien

The Desert Store Book Series:

1. Cowboy Johnson's Desert Oasis
   Mama and the '57 Mercury
2. The Red Cactus Desert
   Geena and the '59 Dodge Lancer
3. The Three Cactus Limbo
   Bud's Garage and the Quest of the
   Three Magi
4. Susan Sugar Diamond
   Away in a Desert
5. The Desert Store
   The Red Cactus Orphanage
6. Manfred's Folly
   Timmon's Legacy
7. The Points of Light

More books by Patsy Stanley:

Addition Jones
An Older Wine
The Color Blue of the Hermit's Robe
Emerald Hawks Flight
Avalon Blue's Quest
Christmas Stories from the Crone's Castle
Big Al's Christmas Wedding
The Dreadful Noises of Landoshar

Chirpy and Cheep Cheep's Montana
Adventure
Laundromat Girl
Billy Silly Beak and Pearl, the Purple Eared Bird
Girl
The Whuzzles
Tom the Owl
The Rebel Bedats
The Blue Rubber Albatross
Benny Berman's Lighthouse
The Amazing Adventures of Chef Pepper King
And Sir Basil Soupstone in The Case of the
Disappearing Spy Cat

The Skaters
Red Leaf
The Green Mountain Shaman
The Mental Body
The Spiritual Nature of Atomic Structure
Sound Energies
Shield Energies
Chakras, Meridians, and the Color Energies
The Elements

Book #7 in the Desert Store series:

The Points of Light

A war is going to be fought. There comes a Time when the Light must rise-and when it does, it doesn't call only the mighty. It calls the odd, the broken, and the ordinary souls who carry special gifts. In this story, the Desert Store misfits answer the Call to defend the Good. Called to defend five different energy vortexes including the Desert store, the misfits and others who are called to join them fight a battle without guns or ammo, or swords. They fight instead with plants. Following mother Earths directions, they fight an unforgettable battle for Good.

Avery, the quiet owner of the Desert Store is back from the dead and protecting the positive-Good energy chakra the Desert store sits on.

From William the Dude, always watching from a distance, Lily Jean Bloome searching the maps, Normaine and Eddy, building warm red courage in everyone, Timmon, with his sense of smell and palate, and Gordon, mime and magician, they begin to gather.

Shem walking the old path barefoot in the east, finding Miz Wind and Marisong. Beck and Hattie holding the line in the west with forest and house. Susan Sugar Diamond, Matthew, Perry and Lana- on the move towards Kansas without knowing why. And in Carolina, Geena and Celia, waking at night to the sound of a woman's voice, singing from the sea, calling them.

Justice doesn't always wear a crown. It can show up in dented pickup trucks, cracked voices, and hands that have seen rough work. The people you'll meet in this story don't look like hero's. They Desert Store misfits are often quirky, sometimes off the wall. Unsung hero's, they answered the call, bringing their odd, every day skills and lifting them to the sacred.